Cubanita

Also by

GABY TRIANA

Backstage Pass

Cubanita

GABY TRIANA

HarperCollins*Publishers*

YA
TRI

www.harperchildrens.com

Library of Congress Cataloging-in-Publication Data
Triana, Gaby.
    Cubanita / by Gaby Triana.— 1st ed.
        p.   cm.
    Summary: Seventeen-year-old Isabel, eager to leave Miami
to attend the University of Michigan and escape her over-
protective Cuban mother, learns some truths about her
family's past and makes important decisions about the type
of person she wants to be.
    ISBN 0-06-056020-7 — ISBN 0-06-056021-5 (lib. bdg.)
    [1. Identity—Fiction. 2. Mothers and daughters—Fiction.
3. Cuban-Americans—Fiction. 4. Interpersonal relations—
Fiction. 5. Miami (Fla.)—Fiction.] I. Title.
PZ7.T7334Cu 2005   2004018462
[Fic]—dc22   CIP
                                                             AC

Typography by Sasha Illingworth
1 2 3 4 5 6 7 8 9 10

First Edition

For Mom and Dad

Cubanita

cubanita \koo-bah-*nee*-tah\ *n*

1: a girl or woman of Cuban descent
   who embraces her culture
2: a Cuban-American girl or woman
   who remains connected to her roots

(antonym) Isabel Díaz

One

She wants me to be her, but I'm not her. I'm not Miss *Cubanita*.

I mean, I love my mom and everything, but I've never even *been* to Cuba, so how can she expect me to embrace it? *This* is my country, the U.S. 'tis of thee, with purple mountains and all that.

Okay, fine, so Miami is basically North Cuba, but still.

Guantanamera . . . guajira guantanamera . . . 1140 AM, WQBA. As if there weren't a thousand other radio stations she could have on.

"Mami, could you please listen to something else? They play that song, like, eighteen times a day." I can't concentrate on my teachers' handbook. I've read the same paragraph three times already.

"*Ay, mi hijita,* it's better than that stuff you listen to that goes *taka-tun, taka-tun, taka-tun*, and makes the car windows shake at every red light. *Esa basura,"* she says, chopping up onions and peppers for the *sofrito* going into our dinner.

"Garbage? Mom, that's what people listen to now. Nobody listens to "Guantanamera." Only a *cubanita* like you, who's stuck in her own little world. Can't you try to act like the American citizen you are? I mean, it's embarrassing. You haven't been to Cuba in twenty-five years. What are you holding on for?"

Ten seconds of painful silence.

Then, "*Sí*, ah-hah, Isabelita. You keep telling yourself you're not Cuban, even though you are. *La verdad que* sometimes I wonder if they didn't switch you for another baby at the hospital. *Qué acomplejada tú eres."*

She hacks the onions with a little more force, shaking her head, then starts talking to herself—the all-time Cuban mother thing to do—to make me feel guilty about not understanding her. "*Ella quiere que yo deje de ser cubana, que deje de pensar en mi país, en mis raíces, en mí . . . "*

I'm outta here. There's no way I can focus with her calling me *acomplejada*. I do not have a complex. Aren't seniors supposed to feel liberated after graduation? Then why am I so suffocated?

I leave the kitchen counter behind, her voice trailing off like one of those slow trucks that announces shrimp for sale in our neighborhood when it disappears around the corner. Doesn't matter what she's saying anyway. It's probably "In Cuba, things were like this, in Cuba, things were like that, in

Cuba, blah, blah, blah." *Ay*, all she ever talks about is Cuba!

In the hallway I pause to look at the oversized photo of me in my *quinceañera* dress. It was the tackiest ball gown you can possibly imagine: ruffles, bows, you name it. My mother insisted I have one of these galas for my fifteenth birthday, arguing tradition and culture keep families strong, but I never felt more alienated from her in my life. I would've rather waited and had a small party for my sixteenth, like half the girls I went to school with, but I caved in to her idea instead. It meant more to her anyway.

·   I remember shopping for THE dress. She wanted poofy; I wanted streamlined. She wanted the dorky studio portrait; I wanted the quick snapshot with the disposable camera. To make a long story short, here it is—a poster of me in a bubble-sleeved dress, wearing a tiara, looking like a teenage bride. So much for trying to compromise with her. All this just for turning a year older. And to please Mami.

Always to please Mami.

Summer just started and already I can't wait to get out of here to begin my mother-free life at the University of Michigan in August. But until that happens, I'll be teaching art at Everglades National Park, same as last year. It has a summer camp—Camp Anhinga, sort of an answer to those Camp Hiawathas up north, except the kids leave at 4:30 P.M. instead of sleep over. I love working there, probably because I've always dreamed of living somewhere other than Miami, somewhere with mountains and resorts.

I start tomorrow, and Mom is anything but thrilled.

Surprise, surprise. If it weren't for my father, who's completely chill about everything, she'd never let me go. Are you kidding? Her *niñita*? Out there, with all those *cocodrilos* waiting for Isabel Díaz to fall in the canal so they can eat her for lunch? Thank God for Dad, that's all I can say. If it weren't for him, I'd never get to experience college away from home. I'd be stuck, taking classes locally, learning to cook and sew the holes in my brother's underwear on the side, cultivating my domestic skills as a backup career. Because that's what a good *cubanita* does, you know, thinks of nothing but home. Yeah. Okay.

Tap, tap.

Always, just as I'm getting ready for bed. "What?"

Tap, tap. My brother thrives on being annoying. You'd think he was younger than me, not twenty-one.

"What do you want, fool?" CK Eternity wafts in under the closed door. "It's unlocked," I say.

The door unlatches slowly, and there stands my brother, Mr. Calvin Klein poster boy, dressed to impress. He's wearing something he obviously just brought home, judging from his fashion show stance. Dark pants and a chocolate, long-sleeved, V-neck crew. Nice, if you live anywhere that actually experiences cool weather instead of eternal heat. He smiles devilishly and spins around. "Eh? Awesome, right? Am I ready to party or what?"

"Stefan, you look like a walking billboard. People don't really dress like that here, doofus—"

"Listen to you," he interrupts. *"People don't really dress like that*. And how would you know? Oh, I forget, you go out so much, you're the Trend Tracker, the Clubhopper. For your info, people do dress like this. And even if they don't, *I* dress like this." He checks his watch.

"Okay, Enrique Iglesias, what I was going to say is that you're gonna get heatstroke the moment you step into any club. Remember, ninety degrees outside means, like, a hundred and ninety inside."

"Oh, *la experta*," he says, faking awe at my knowledge. "Isa, who gives a shit? I'll sweat, it don't matter, 'cause I look good, baby!" He cries with glee, hopping in front of the mirror, smoothing back his dark hair.

He's right. It doesn't matter. Stefan'll get the chicks anyway. He always does. A bit of discomfort is a small price to pay for getting laid.

"Very true," I say, eyeing the red clearance tag on the back of his pants. $12.99. I hold back a killer laugh. "Nothing's more important than looking sharp. Go get 'em, macho man."

He smiles big, approving of my change in attitude. "There you go!" Leaning over me in bed, he kisses my forehead. And out he goes to scout, like a shark in a coral reef.

In the morning, the usual smells wake me. My mother's kitchen . . . a virtual alarm clock. After getting dressed in my work uniform of khakis and a bright green polo shirt, I grab my handbook and shove it into my bag. Out to face the day. But first I have to get past Breakfast Security.

"*Mi vida, un poquito de café con leche, ¿anda?*" Mom implores when I rush into the kitchen. She holds up a cup of coffee with milk for me. I can see she's also made *tostada*—a flattened, grilled, loaded-with-butter slice of bread. Reading the newspaper while standing at the counter, my father downs his breakfast without a word.

Do I break her heart or take the offering? Today's high is supposed to be around ninety-eight degrees, yet she's holding her mug close to her like a blizzard's blowing outside. I laugh. Too funny. "Mami, do you realize it's too hot for coffee? I'll just take some OJ instead."

She sighs and tries to hand me the plate with crunchy *tostada*. "*Bueno*, at least eat this, *toma*." Actually it does smell good.

"Mom, I gotta go. I'll take it with me, okay?" I open the fridge and pour some juice into a travel mug.

"Fine." She wraps it up in a Wendy's napkin and hands it to me. Only my mother would grab a stack of thirty Wendy's napkins before exiting the restaurant. One can never have enough of those suckers. God forbid she put the toast in a Baggie like everyone else. "Eat it in the car, Isa. Don't eat it at the camp, because you know *como son los cocodrilos*."

I watch my dad hold back a smile.

"Mami," I say, turning away from my dad before I start laughing, "the alligators don't just come up to people and grab toast out of their hands. If they did, the park wouldn't allow tourists to walk up to them when they're out of the water."

She lightly scratches my dad's back, like she's been doing for the last twenty-five years. "*Mi hijita*, listen to your mother. *Los cocodrilos muerden.*"

"They do not bite, Mom. Not for no reason anyway. But the panthers . . . the panthers like to attack the tour trams when they drive by." I wink at my dad. He winks back. "I'll call you at lunchtime."

"*¿Besito?*" She turns out her cheek, a hundred *tostada* crumbs sprinkled across it, like a two-year-old waiting for a kiss.

Ah, Mami. I laugh.

"*¿De qué te ríes?*" she asks, unamused by my snickering.

"Nothing! I'm not laughing at you. Bye, Mami." I kiss her and squeeze her soft hand. It looks more like a teenager's than one belonging to a fifty-year-old mother of three. "Bye, Daddy." I kiss him, too, and he grunts in return.

"*¿De qué te ríes?*" she asks again, her voice following me out to the foyer.

"I'm not laughing at anything. Bye, Mami. *Límpiate aquí,*" I tell her, mock-wiping my cheek.

"*¡Fresca!*" She says with a huff, finally flinging the crumbs away.

Okay, so my mom and I *do* get along sometimes. She can be funny and goofy and generous, when she's not talking about Cuba. How she can spend so much energy discussing a place that plays human rights like pawns in a game of chess is beyond me. I just don't get it. Outside, I take my red, white, and blue Mickey Mouse ornament off my truck's antenna and transfer it over to hers. There, that should remind her where she's living. Duh, wait. Cuba's flag has the same colors. Oh, I'll leave it. This one has stars on it.

My house is practically in the Everglades, so it's a short drive to camp in the mornings. No traffic out on Tamiami Trail. Nobody heading to the River of Grass at 7:00 A.M. Only tourists looking for airboat rides and me in the old Chevy. With the windows down, the aroma of the saw grass, humidity, and morning air whipping my face, I can't help but think that these scents will always remind me of home, no matter where I go, no matter where I end up living years from now.

As I drive up to the camp's main house, I see Susy, my work buddy, waving at me, a giddy look on her face. In the two years I've been working with her, I've learned what that look means. There's fresh meat on campus—a new man.

Behind her I spot him, also wearing the camp's uniform. About twenty maybe, like Susy. Strong legs, tall, watching me as I pull into a parking space. Nice arms! I see the boy takes his vitamins. Jonathan, the camp's assistant (read: wanna-be) director, yaps away with this mystery man, no doubt briefing him on his duties, except Mystery Man half ignores him. Instead his intense gaze follows me, like one of those ghostly busts at the Haunted Mansion at Disney World.

And so begins my final summer at Camp Anhinga. This should be interesting.

Two

It's not even 7:30 in the morning, but the heat's already burned the mist off the swamp's surface. A single egret greets me at its edge, eyeing me closely as I approach the camp's main building. Maybe it remembers me from last year. Maybe it's the same one from my blue-ribbon painting I exhibited at the Youth Fair, asking to pose again in exchange for a brown snail. Okay, maybe not.

Two steps behind me, Susy flutters like a big, grinning moth. "Did you see him?"

"See who?" Mystery Man. Of course I saw that chiseled perfection.

"You're kidding. Did the split with Robi impair your vision as well as your judgment?"

"Ha, ha, very funny." Another person who thinks I was warped when I cut the guy loose a month ago. "Susy, the whole reason for breaking up with Robi was to clean the slate before leaving for U-M. I'm not looking at another guy this summer. I don't want to be involved with anyone right now."

"Involved?" She snorts. "Who said anything about getting involved? I was only asking if you saw that ass. You know exactly who I'm talking about. Your eyes went superwide. And by the way, you might want to stop saying U-M. Everybody thinks you mean University of Miami."

"Whatever."

There he is again. Weird, his face isn't that good-looking, not pretty boy anyway. More serious, rugged, with piercing dark eyes. Still, he'd qualify as good-looking in that ugly sort of way. You know exactly what I mean. This time he's trying harder not to stare at me, but quick glances escape him, as Susy and I go by.

"Ladies," Jonathan booms in a voice full of upper hierarchy. "Come hither." If only our real director would come out of his office every now and then, we wouldn't have to deal with Dorkus Erectus here.

We head up the sidewalk. On a cypress branch, about fifteen yards behind Jonathan, there's an anhinga drying itself off after a morning fish, its wingspan extending against the pink sky. But as we get closer, it also looks like it's sitting right on top of Jon's head. A glorious crown to an unsuspecting, doofus totem pole.

"What is it?" Jonathan asks, noticing my smile.

Mystery Man doesn't get it either. He's kind of scowling, although I'm starting to think maybe that's his normal expression. The frown brings out his eyes, deep brown, rimmed with dark long lashes—lashes I'd kill for. Why do men always get the Cover Girl look naturally, when I need mascara? I tell you.

"Nothing," I say. Like I'm about to tell Jon there seems to be a huge wading bird perched on his head. Too bad it's not really sitting on him. I'd give anything to see it poop on the King of Control Freaks. "What's up?"

Beside me, Susy's zeroing in on Mystery Man. She straightens herself, puffing up her chest, doing her best to show the new guy what a real woman's made of.

Jonathan gives us a forced smile. "Just wanted you to meet Andrew Corbin."

Andrew. Great name. I bet I could count on one hand the number of South Floridians who don't cringe at the mention of it. Even though it's been eons since the storm tore through here.

"Coach Andrew," Mystery Man kindly interrupts, finally breaking out a weak smile.

Ah, coach. Hence the underwear ad physique. "Cool," I say cleverly. Wait, I thought we already had an activities coach. Coach Ig was at the first meeting last week, and this guy wasn't. "Iggy's gone?"

"Yeah, he left. Found something better, I guess," Jonathan scoffs. "So the field belongs to Andrew."

"Really?" Susy tucks her tongue into her cheek, and her eyelashes sweep over Coach Andrew like some huge plumy feathers. "That's exciting. Awesome, really."

I look at her with golf ball eyes, and if she pays close attention, she can see *clueless* written all over my face. But she doesn't. Because she's clueless.

Andrew grins like he's comfortable with this dumb display of raging estrogen. I guess the girls-gone-gaga thing happens to him a lot.

"So, ladies . . . make sure Andrew's up to speed with all the house rules, all right?" Jon spots the parade of yellow and black swamp buggies starting to invade the parking lot. "Buses are here. Gotta go." He trudges off to exercise his control freakiness at the registration desk.

Andrew, Susy, and I stroll toward the entrance of the main house. They'll need us to take our groups in about fifteen minutes.

"Yeah, this is awesome." Andrew picks up on Susy's unabashed enthusiasm. "Iggy's been talking about this camp for a while now. Said I could probably hook up here for the summer."

"Excuse me?" Susy asks, lusty fog obviously clouding her judgment.

"Work here. I meant hook up, as in 'work here.'" He smiles.

"Oh." Susy meant hook up, as in "find a piece of ass," but whatever. I guess she's smitten, even if his face *does* fall within the intimidating-ugly-yet-somehow-attractive category.

"You know Iggy?" she asks.

"Ig? Yeah, we were roommates last year, but I got my own

place now. He's working at the bookstore this summer."

Ohhhh, Andrew knows Iggy from UM. The other UM. The one my mother would rather I go to, the one only a few miles away, not as far up the continental U.S. from her as possible.

I try to catch Susy's expression. She dated Iggy for a month, and obviously never learned about Andrew, judging from her clucking tongue. Let's get this ball between them rolling already. "Andrew," I say cheerfully, "this is my friend Susana. She teaches science."

He looks at her like she's nothing more than a little old lady or an office buddy of his father's. "Hey, Susana," he says, offering his hand.

"Susy," she replies breathlessly, taking it in hers.

"Susy." He smiles at her again, but it's a polite smile, not a how-you-doin', wanna-shag-now-or-shag-later smile. His gaze keeps flitting over to me. "And you're . . . ?"

"Sorry. Isabel . . . Isa. Nice to have you along for the ride."

Susy coughs into her fist and smiles, no doubt envisioning Coach Andrew as a wild ride.

"Along for the summer," I correct. "That's cool. Good luck." Whew.

I leave them both and head for the buses. One by one, the little darlings jump off the bottom steps, toting their cute backpacks, eager to learn about Everglades ecology. One of them, a teeny girl with a long swishing ponytail decorated with a green ribbon, bounces to the ground and spots Andrew. "Andy! Andy!"

Coach Andrew turns around, a silly grin materializing on

his face, lighting up his whole being. "Hey, chicken-chickee!" He crouches low, and the flying child comes swooping in, landing beautifully in his open arms.

She hugs him close, smiling into his shoulder. Then she plants a sweet kiss on his cheek and coos, "Where's Iggy?"

"Iggy's not here anymore. But I am," he says softly, tickling her ribs until she squeals in delight. "Ig's niece," he offers to Susy as an explanation, then takes off with Chicken-Chickee to the registration desk.

I'm completely stunned. Not sure why. It's just that I don't know anything about this Andrew. I guess because of his hard stare, I thought he was the serious type, a jerk even, into his own ego. But if a little girl with a swishing ponytail and ribbon in her hair can run up to him the way this one did, and smother him the way this one did, and laugh all bubbly with him like this one did, then he can't be all that bad. In fact, he's gotta be pretty great, right?

As they enter the building hand in hand, I catch myself smiling openly.

I stroll around the art room, helping my seven-year-olds draw monarch butterflies. One of my students, a stocky little girl with shiny blond hair, tugs on my shirt. "Ms. Díaz?"

"Yes?" I smile.

She points her black crayon at a wide-eyed boy next to her. "He's bothering me."

I can't possibly see how this poor boy can be bothering her. He looks like Bambi, for Christ's sake. But there—it took a whole twenty minutes for the kids to start telling on one another. That's the only thing I don't like about this job.

"Bothering you? Why . . ." I look down at my clipboard. "Yessica, he's just sharing the crayons with you. You have to share, sweetie."

Yessica looks about as thrilled at hearing this as, say, a cat going in for a flea bath. She sighs. "Fine. But only because you knew my name. And because you're pretty."

"Oh." I touch my hair for some reason.

"You look like that lady with the brown hair and brown eyes from that commercial about the shampoo that they play when my mom is watching that program she watches."

No clue what she's talking about, but if I look like anyone in any hair product commercial, that's good, I guess. "Well. Thank you. Yessica. That's very nice of you."

Now, why didn't Robi ever tell me things like that?

During lunch, Susy's baffled. "Why didn't Iggy ever mention Andrew? I mean, hello, they were roommates."

"Why are you surprised? Don't you think Iggy knew what he was doing by not introducing you two? You would've traded him for Andrew in a heartbeat. He knew that." I guess Iggy wasn't as dense as I thought. "Besides, you guys only went out for a month." Sex. That's all Susy wanted from him anyway.

No answer, as she bites into a bologna and cheese sandwich.

At 4:30, the first day wraps up smoothly. No accidents,

tantrums, or barfing. No children eaten by ferocious alligators. Mami will be disappointed. My afternoon kids worked with watercolors wonderfully, better than I expected. Minimum spillage and a surprising sense of impressionism for second graders. Best of all, it's been a peaceful day away from home.

But every time I turned a corner today, walking the kids to their next activity, I felt a presence. As much as I tried to avoid it, I knew that Andrew's gaze was fixed on me from the PE field, dark eyes following me from underneath his baseball cap.

Though it should feel a bit creepy, a part of me is satisfied that someone actually bypassed Susy's "take me, I put out" antics and noticed me instead. For once. So I find myself smiling for the second time today.

Home less than a minute, I already hear the kitchen radio blaring the daily specials at Sedano's supermarket, and my mother begins invading my personal space. "*¿Ey, casi las seis? ¿Cómo te fue? ¿Qué hicieron?*" She heaves a basket of laundry onto the living room sofa. She's trying hard not to be intrusive, asking only three questions rather than the usual twenty.

"I'm late because there was traffic, it went fine, and the kids loved my lessons. How was *your* day, Mami?"

She sighs heavily and drops next to the basket to begin folding. "You didn't call, Isa."

"Sorry, Mom. It was a busy first day." I plop down next to

her and begin matching socks.

She whips a T-shirt into shape, then transforms it into a perfectly folded rectangle. "*Stefanito se fue a la playa con Oscarito*. He hasn't called all day either."

Stefanito. His friend Oscarito. My mother must make everything diminutive. It can't just be Stefan . . . no, it's gotta be Little Stefan. Not Oscar, Little Oscar.

"Yeah, but if Stefan's been at the beach all day, he should've called you. It's not like he's working. I mean, at least *I'm* working."

"*Sí, mi vida*, but he's a man," she says matter-of-factly.

"Huh?" I blurt, as if I'm not used to this double standard by now. "What's that supposed to mean? Because he's a guy, he doesn't have to call you? Besides, Stefan's hardly a man, Mami. What does he do all day? Go to the beach? Shop? That's being a man?"

She flips up a palm. "*Mi hija, no empieces.*"

Don't start, she says. Here I am, using my precious time to make something of myself, working for a living, preparing for college, only to get Mami's grief for everything I do. But Stefan! Stefan takes two classes a week at Miami-Dade and earns her respect anyway, just because he's got testicles? Please! My brother's a bum. Mami should be giving *him* grief, but she doesn't because he's Prince Stefanito, the prized boy in the family, the spicy ham neatly sandwiched between two unappreciative slices of white bread.

Speaking of which, my sister hasn't written me in a few days. "I'm gonna go change," I tell Mom, heading to my room to check e-mail.

In the solace of my four walls, I look through messages and find one from my sis. Carmen's twenty-five and managed to escape my mother's talons by going to Valdosta State, marrying a non-Hispanic American, and working as a nurse *waaaay* far from home in Virginia. How she did it, I'm not sure. Probably because my dad vetoed Mom's suggestion that Carmen stay home to sew underwear. *Go*, he said, *dream and pursue happiness*. Mom wasn't as happy after that. Not that I enjoy my mother being unhappy, but Carmen is my hero. Go, Carmen!

From: C. Díaz-Sanders
To: Isabelita
Subject: Congratulations!

Hi, baby girl! It kills me that I couldn't go to your graduation, but since I just started at St. Jude's, I couldn't take any days off. I'll be sure to use my first vacation days visiting you at school. Did you get the graduation card I sent? There's a check inside. Use it wisely. Like I even have to tell you that.

Ready to leave? Don't worry, August will be here before you know it, then you'll be free! Yay! God, I can't believe my little sis is going off to college! That's awesome, mamita. Good for you. Bueno, hang in there. Love Mami and Papi, but be yourself. Don't give in to ancient notions.

Love you,
Carmen
P.S. Dan says hi.

I reply, telling Carmen about Mom, camp, and Andrew. Carmen always has a way of making me feel empowered. I miss her. But I can understand why she left. Mami's a great mom, don't get me wrong. She's smart and funny and fiercely protective of her family, but she's . . . overwhelming sometimes. Makes you want to go somewhere, like Virginia, and just breathe.

After dinner, "alone" would be a good word to describe the way I feel. No one here seems to understand the things I want out of life. College, a career in art, independence. Carmen comes closest, but she's over nine hundred miles away. Robi understood too, but no need to call and confuse him. Here at home, however, the people to click with are running thin.

Even Susy is now preoccupied with Hurricane Andrew— whose daunting gaze is the last thing I remember before dozing off to sleep.

Three

Look at those clouds. A storm brewing over the Everglades—how timeless. The same cycle, century after century, is such a phenomenon. Rain falls, lightning strikes, fires start, then we come in and ruin it all by trying to put them out. Amazing, all nature's trying to do is burn the old to make room for the new, but we see that as bad. Maybe the human race is destined to self-destruct. Maybe I'm too cynical for my age, like Mami says. Maybe I need to quit staring out the window and add brighter colors to this painting.

White, white, where's my white? Ah, there it is.

It's been two weeks since the first day of camp. Coach Andrew has greeted me from afar every day this week, a mere wave from across the PE field, and that's it. I guess he's just a nice guy, although the fact that his face was the last thing I thought of that first night is unnerving. Why am I even thinking about him? It's not like he swept me off my feet or anything, or like he's that cute, either. Susy's the one who should be dreaming about him, not me. I'm not looking at guys this summer, not even Robi.

For real, I'm not.

Mmm. Is it unnatural to love the smell of oils and turpentine this much?

Roberto Puertas. We've known each other since elementary school and were a couple for the last two years. Everything was fine. He's a nice guy from a great family, Cuban-American like me, so we understood each other pretty well. Not only is he a good person, he is gifted in the looks department too. So why dump him?

Well, here's the thing. He was starting to talk seriously about me as "Mrs. Puertas." I mean, hi, hello, we're seventeen. Granted, he didn't mean for another few years, until after college graduation, but still. I'd like to get married one day, but it's too far away to even think about. What am I supposed to do? Nurture a long-distance relationship come August? I don't think so. He's a great guy, but Robi can look for someone else to sew his underwear. Case closed.

This painting's coming out pretty good. It's one of my better oils. A girl about my age, back facing the viewer. She's looking out at . . . okay, I haven't decided what yet, but I hope to create a sense of sadness, like she's longing for something. I want the viewer to wonder about it and identify with her. The hard part is evoking that kind of emotion without being able to see her face. But that's what I love about painting.

As I'm detailing the creases of her linen shirt, I hear the door to the art room quietly creak open. It could easily be the wind from the impending rain, but you know how you can sense when someone walks into a room, even when they're real quiet? It's an air displacement thing. Well, I look over and see guess who? Coach.

"Hey." He admires the room from the doorway.

"How's it going so far? Come in. Everybody treating you okay?" My God, there's that haunting look again. Someone should use him in a horror movie. But then, he's got that solid form that could earn him a role in a baseball flick. About six foot two, but not too pumped up. Got a natural build. Which I like.

Which I like? Isa! What was all that rationalizing for, not five minutes ago?

Andrew chooses to remain in the doorway. "Everything's going great. I was just packing up to go home, thought I'd check out the whole facility for once. Haven't been in here yet."

"The art room? Oh, it's nice. Nothing too exciting, but it's home to me. Closets, colored paper, glue bottles, that kind of stuff. No volleyballs in here." I laugh.

He's not laughing. "I wasn't looking for volleyballs anyway."

Oh.

"Have you seen Susy?" I ask cheerfully, hoping he'll remember the highly available bimbette buddy of mine and leave me alone. Maybe he should be wandering into her lab, where kids get to look at bass eggs under microscopes.

"Yeah, she was talking to a parent a little while ago. I didn't know she's the same Susy that dated Iggy. Weird."

"I know, right? She didn't know you were his roommate. Such a small world."

He nods in agreement.

I nod.

We stand there nodding. I go back to my painting before adding, "Why'd you move out? You guys had a tiff?"

"With Iggy?" He plays with the doorknob, turning and letting it bounce back to its original position. "Nah, nothing happened. He's a cool guy. I love his family. They practically adopted me when I moved in with him. I just always wanted my own place, I guess, and I found an awesome apartment right across from campus."

Ah, he wanted his own shag pad. Can't blame him. "Oh, well, hey. Gotta follow your dreams, right? You gonna come in?"

He pulls his equipment bag behind him and leans it against the wall. Then he starts strolling around quietly, contemplating the kids' watercolor landscapes hung up to dry. "What's this one?" He points to one with darker shades than the others.

"Those aren't finished. They're backgrounds only, but my guess is a thunderstorm over land."

"Really?" He leans in and squints. "How can you see that? I just see gray on the top and brown on the bottom."

"I don't know. That's just what I see."

He examines it again.

"So where do you live?" I ask, then remember. "Forget it, right off campus."

"Yeah. Originally I'm from Daytona Beach. Grew up there. But now my family's in Orlando, and I'm here. I'm a junior, starting business classes in the fall."

"Business? That's cool. I don't have a head for business, but I admire people who do. Like my dad. He runs a great company and everybody really looks up to him."

"What company?"

"You've probably never heard of it. ISC Communications."

"Hmmm, nope. You're right." He laughs. "Never heard of it. What's the ISC stand for?"

"Actually it's just the initials of my name, my brother Stefan's, and my sister Carmen's."

He chuckles, inching his way to my easel. "Your dad sounds like a cool guy."

"He is," I answer rather quickly. "He is. Maybe you can talk to him sometime."

"Yeah? That'd be cool if I ever decide to start my own company. He could give me some pointers." Andrew finishes perusing the kids' paintings. He approaches my corner of the room, sneakers scuffing softly across the concrete floor. He looks comfortable, even though he's alone with someone he doesn't know in the slightest. Me, I'm trying real hard not to show how intimidated I'm feeling right about now.

But then the memory of Andrew that first day, arms open to Iggy's flying niece, sneaks into my mind. The way he completely changed, how he was Mystery Man one second, then sweet Uncle Andy the next, and I'm suddenly fine. I'd judged him too quickly. I thought he was full of himself. But she hugged him so lovingly, she even kissed his cheek.

Finally he arrives at my easel and quietly watches me work. "That's incredible," he says, and, if I'm not mistaken, he drew a breath before saying it.

"Thanks. It's not finished, but thanks." That's awfully nice of him, but I can hear my mom's unwelcome voice in my head. *Este huevo quiere sal.* This guy's on to something, so watch out.

He stands there frozen, while I use a fine point to create the folds on the girl's shirt catching the breeze. Ocean. She's going to be looking out at the ocean, I've just decided. There's a storm on the horizon just like the one outside. We breathe quietly for a minute.

"God, that's so amazing how you do that. I can't even draw stick figures. You, you just paint life exactly the way it is. That's so cool."

"Wow, thanks," I say again, too embarrassed to look at him. I pretend to be absorbed by my work, talking to him only to be polite, but the truth is I don't want to see his face. I don't want to see those lashes batting over those eyes. What if I see something in them I don't want to? What if they're telling me something I don't want to know?

"Isabel," he says softly, moving in to see the painting close-up, "this girl, she sorta looks like a puppy waiting for someone to come home. Someone she's been waiting for, right?"

Silence.

I was hoping for a more open interpretation with this piece, but this nonartisan business major just hit the bull's-eye. "Um . . . yeah. That's what I was aiming for. Very good, Coach." I say it casually, but I'm almost too stunned to move. Coach Andrew surprises me yet again. I thought he was about to ask me out, but I obviously know little about him. And here's the scary part—I want to know more.

"I'm sorry," he says, floating closer to me, sensing my amazement. "Was I not supposed to guess that yet?"

I pull the brush away from the canvas, dipping the point into the little vat of turpentine, swishing to clean off the paint. I wipe the bristles on a paper towel and place the brush upright into a cup. "No, that's great. That's exactly what I was hoping people would think." I wipe my hands on my apron. Why are they sweating? Then, without thinking, I do it. I look at him.

A split second later, butterflies flutter inside me. Andrew is closing the space between us. He creeps in to look at the painting, but my mind imagines something else, something I don't even want to think about. I swore to myself I wouldn't. Beneath heavy brows, his dark eyes search my face. I can feel myself swooning. Butterflies are one thing, but swooning? I've never swooned with anybody. Not even Robi.

Andrew smiles. A big, beautiful smile. A sexy smile, damn him. Damn him! What is wrong with me?

He glances down at his shoe and kicks the floor with his

heel. "Hey, would it be okay if we got together outside this place? Maybe hang out somewhere? I'd love to talk more, but we don't have much time here."

My response gets stuck on delay. *Um . . . um.* In the distance, a rumble of thunder fills in the silence, and a whooping crane cries out.

Andrew, sensing a refusal on the brink, adds, "If not, it's okay. I can take a no."

No to Underwear Ad Guy? I don't think so. So we'll go out, no big deal. I can go out with someone as long as I don't get too involved, right? "Yeah, sure. That'd be great," I hear myself say, right as the image of Susy's gaping mouth flits through my mind.

"Awesome." He smiles again, and I swear that now, he's extremely hot. That scowl isn't so bad, actually. His attitude and everything else make up for it. He looks again at my painting. "What does she want? The girl."

"The girl?" *Oh, right, the girl.* "I'm not sure, really."

I haven't the foggiest idea, but I guess she's gotta want something.

"Maybe we'll figure it out over coffee." He punches my arm playfully, a magical smile gracing his face. Goofy Uncle Andy.

"Maybe," I say, having a hard time ignoring the vision of myself as Chicken-Chickee, with the swishing ponytail, running into his arms.

Four

From: Roberto Puertas
To: Isa Díaz
Subject: Hey, Isa

How've you been? What have you been up to? Remember that I'm always here for you if you need me. Call me anytime. I haven't seen your face ringing on my camera phone in a while. Remember how it used to crack me up after school during band practice?

Robi

I don't reply. Instead, I close all windows and log off. He just wants to see if I'm home. I check myself in the mirror one last time and head out to the living room.

"*¿A dónde vas?*" my mom asks as soon as she sees me.

"*Déjala.*" From behind the *TV Guide*, my dad tells Mami to give me a break.

I clear my throat and prepare for the onslaught. "I don't know where we're going yet, Mami. Probably somewhere to get coffee. That's what he mentioned."

"*¿Mi vida, por qué te estás enredando en algo nuevo?*"

"What? I'm not getting wrapped up in anything new. I'm just going to have coffee with a fellow teacher."

"On a Thursday night, *hija?*"

"So?"

"I thought it was too hot for coffee."

Oh, now she thinks she's funny, just because I haven't been drinking hers in the morning. Mom could've been an accountant with that scorekeeping of hers. She offers her best disapproving smirk. "*¿Y vestida así?*"

"*Déjala,*" my dad referees again, without a glance our way.

I look down at the outfit I threw on. Fine, the one I chose carefully. My superlow jeans with a really cute blue peasant top, which Stefan picked out for me. I guess it's not so bad having a mall rat for a brother. "What's wrong with what I'm wearing?"

"Is that how everyone dresses when meeting a fellow *teasher?*"

I make a huge effort to avoid rolling my eyes. "It's teacher, Mami, not *teasher*. Honestly, I don't know why you can't say teacher. It's the same *ch*-sound as in *chocolate*. You can say *chocolate* just fine, can't you? So say teacher."

"¡Teacher . . . *teasher* . . . *déjame tranquila ya!*" She flails the remote control high above her head. And God also forbid she could speak without using the full range of her arms.

"*Teasher* is something you wear with jeans," I add. If grief is what she wants to give me tonight, two can play that game.

"Isa, enough." My dad's crooked eyebrow warns from above the magazine.

You know, she came here when she was nineteen. It's been, like, twenty-six years. You'd think in twenty-six years, she could learn how to speak correctly. "Look, this is what I'm wearing, okay? There's nothing wrong with it."

She quickly scans my ensemble before focusing back on Univision. "He's going to get the wrong impression."

"Mom, stop it! I'm not wearing a see-through teddy, am I?"

"*Para de gritar*," she calmly orders.

"I'm not screaming."

"*Para de gritar*," she coos, and any moment now, I probably *will* scream, just from hearing her ask me *not* to.

"*Déjala*," my father says yet again.

See what I mean? I can't take this! I just love the way she picks fights, pushing all the right buttons, then asks me to stay calm. Bullshit! My friends never have to put up with this. Their mothers always let them wear whatever they want, as long as it isn't slutty. Me, I'm wearing the most normal outfit ever, but she puts on a show.

I tell you, if *not* going out with Andrew is what she wants from me tonight, she's doing more harm than good. If there's anything I want, it's to see him. Someone with a fresh face. Someone who'll listen without criticizing. Someone who can

30

pronounce "teacher"!

"Good night, Mom." I think I'll wait for Andrew outside. I grab my keys from my purse and aim for the door. "Good night, Dad."

As I'm walking out, I hear my father blowing his usual good-bye kisses. My mother's voice, icy and stubborn, calls from the living room. *"Isa, no llegues tarde."*

Humpf. I'll get home whatever time I damn well please. Of course, I'd never say that. My father would shove that *TV Guide* right up my ass.

Starbucks on Miracle Mile is crazy. We wait, like, twenty minutes just to order and another five to get our drinks. Still, it's a great night, moon out and everything, as Andrew and I sit outside. Table for two. Lots of people on the sidewalk, probably on their way to the art studios around here. Maybe after I stop boring Andrew with tales of Mother Díaz, we can head to one.

Out of thin air a girl appears at our side. A little older than me, blond and pretty. "Andrew, hi!"

He looks up, his eyes go wide. "Hey, Jenny! What're you up to?"

The navel-ring-baring chick points at a group of giggling girls waiting to cross the street. "Nah, I'm just here with my friends. Came over to say hi." She swivels at the waist like a toddler.

"Cool, this is Isa," he says.

She looks at me for, like, a fraction of a second. "Hi."

"Hi." *Remove thyself from the premises, Blondie.*

Before she can say anything else, Andrew adds, "Great, well, I'll see you around." Kind of a sudden way to end things, but good for him. Fifty points.

"Okay." Jenny smiles in my direction, like she gets the hint, but leans in to give Andrew a quick peck on the cheek anyway. "See you, bye."

Yes, bye-bye, run along and play. "Who's that?" I ask with a smile.

"Girl from school. She lives in my building. Always saying hi, even though I hardly know her."

"Gotcha." I was correct about the girls-gone-gaga thing. This happens to him a lot.

He shrugs and takes a swig of his Grande Caramel Macchiato with skim milk, hold the whipped cream. What's the fun of a macchiato without the whipped cream? Or *whippee creen*, as Mami would say. He twirls a wooden stirring stick in his cup. "Why does she act that way? Your mom."

"My mom? Oh, my mom." I almost forgot what we were talking about before Blondie broke the flow. "Why? Who knows? It defies explanation. I believe researchers are still working on it. They've listed her under Freaks of Nature."

Andrew stares, not sure whether to nod in sympathy or laugh out loud. So I go on, "If you'd like to help the cause, send a donation to the Deciphering Cuban Mothers Fund of Little Havana."

Then he loses it. He cracks up, drawing attention from people at neighboring tables. "You don't even live in Little

Havana!" He covers his face and goes on laughing.

Me, I'm trying hard not to laugh, so he won't think I amuse myself on a regular basis. "You think I'm kidding? I bet you never had to put up with this kind of stuff. I bet your mom's normal, and she gave you free reign over your life while you were home."

Suddenly his laugh dies down. He clears his throat, and an uncomfortable stillness fills the air between us. Uh-oh, what did I say? "Andrew? I'm sorry. Did I just stick my foot in my mouth?"

Looking down, he shakes his head and softly pounds the table with his fist.

I lean in and try to peer into his face. "Andrew? Please don't tell me—"

He looks up, deep brown eyes locking with mine. "My mother died. When I was nine."

"Oh, Andrew." My hand flies to my mouth. "I'm so sorry! I should've thought about that before I said anything. I've only known you a few weeks, and here I am making such a stupid comment! I'm really sorry. Please don't hate me."

He shakes his head some more, biting his lip, but it doesn't look like he's upset, it looks like he's . . . And then he can't hold it anymore. He loses it. He's laughing and snorting, and I'm just an idiot who fell for the oldest trick in the book.

"You jerk!" I chuck a few napkins at him, while he continues to crack himself up. "I can't believe you did that! I felt really bad! I really thought your mother had died."

His face does that thing again, where it goes from intimidating to sunny. He's got the coolest smile ever, wide and sexy. "She lives in Orlando with my dad and little sister. Spends half her time on the Internet and makes Key lime pies the rest of the day."

"You freak!" I pull my earlobe. I always do when I'm nervous. Why am I nervous? There's nothing to be nervous about. Andrew's funny, he's cool, he's . . .

Mi vida, por qué te estás enredando en algo nuevo?

What? Who said that? Great, now I'm hearing Mami's voice again. Shoo, go away!

"Spends half her day on the Internet, then bakes?" I ask, trying to focus on Andrew's explanation. I won't go any farther than that. What if he's kidding again?

"Yeah, she runs a home business. She takes Internet orders, then bakes the meanest Key lime pies you've ever tasted."

"Really? We'll just have to see about that. My mom makes a killer Key lime pie too."

"Your mom? But you make her out to be this flag-waving Cuban lady who'd, if anything, be making flans, not Key lime pies."

"Oh, but she does. Don't get me wrong. She makes a killer flan, too, but I bet you my mother's Key lime pie is better than your mother's Key lime pie."

He fakes injury, looking around to see if other coffee-sippers are listening in on the challenge. "Yeah? Well, I'll have her overnight one tomorrow, then we'll find out who's the real Queen of Key lime."

"Fine." I cross my arms with a grin.

"Fine."

"Your mother doesn't stand a chance." I offer my most childish competitive spirit.

"And yours doesn't stand a *shance*." His lips press together and his eyes open wide, as he awaits any flying objects that may suddenly come his way.

Oh, so now he's mocking my mom? "That's so not funny," I tell him, dead serious.

His expression changes to one of deep concern. "What's not?"

"What you said."

"What? The *shance* thing?"

"Yes."

His eyebrows draw together. "But you made fun of your mom's accent yourself! So now I can't make fun of her?"

"No. *I* can make fun of her. You can't."

"You can't be serious."

No answer.

He watches my face carefully. "Isa, I'm sorry. Really. I was only messing with you."

No answer.

He tilts his head and looks me dead in the eye. I stare back at him, meeting his scowl with my own. Then, I can't help it, and the corners of my lips turn up. He grins big, pointing a long finger straight at my nose, and almost immediately I fall apart. "You almost had me!" he cries.

"Dammit! I can never hold a serious face!" I throw the

napkins at him again, and again, and again. "Jerk! Jerk! Jerk!"

"You almost had me!" he repeats, and in a surprise move, leans in and gathers my hands in his, humming to himself, pleased.

Okay, this is weird. Nice, but weird. So this is what another guy's hands feel like after two years of holding Robi's. Actually, it's more than nice, it's butterfly-inducing. I can handle this. We're just holding hands, no big deal. I lean forward, feeling my arms squeeze my chest, creating a great display of boobage.

He's going to get the wrong impression, my mother's voice echoes in my brain. What the hell? Someone get her out of here! "Shut up," I murmur softly.

"Excuse me?" Andrew's eyebrows sneak up.

"Nothing." I smile.

He glances around, looking for anyone to whom I might be directing my order, then decides it's no one. "You're freaking me out, you know that?" But he smiles again, and I know he's really kidding. Grabbing his paper cup, he downs the rest of the macchiato. "Let's go somewhere."

It's not really a suggestion. It's a declaration. I shrug an okay, toting my half-drunk mocha frap in one hand, hanging on to Andrew with the other.

"Here, take these back to your mom." He pushes the Starbucks napkins toward me on the table. "They're not from Wendy's, but they still work the same."

I laugh again. I'm laughing a lot, aren't I? Who knew such a mean-looking dude could be so goofy? But somewhere in the back of my mind, almost too far to even notice, I realize this laugh was forced. My own thoughts, not Mom's, whisper, *That wasn't funny.*

At Ponce de Leon Boulevard, we stop in front of an art studio packed with loud, appreciative admirers. Andrew and I are still holding hands, so I haven't been able to concentrate on much else. The canvases gracing the walls here are colorful interpretations of Cuban landscapes. A woman holding a tray of tiny cups of Cuban coffee offers us some.

"*No, gracias,*" I decline. That stuff is pure liquid nitro.

We stop in front of a small painting of a *guajiro*, an old countryman, dressed in the traditional white pants and *guayabera* shirt. Red bandanna laced around his shoulders. Wide-brimmed straw hat tilting over a rugged, smiling face. We stand there for a while admiring it.

"That one's awesome," he says. "It looks just like Iggy's father."

I then decide to forgive his little joke earlier. After all, he's a good guy, he likes the *guajiro* painting. A young boy, no older than ten, weaves in and out of the visitors' legs, handing out sheets of neon blue paper. I take one graciously.

CUBA EXPO
Coconut Grove Convention Center
Come and enjoy the sights and sounds of old Cuba!
Reminisce!
August 8–9

On the back, the same thing in Spanish.

Cuba Expo. Mom first went to this fair with Stefan and Dad, like, eight years ago, and has been trying to get me to come along ever since. Says I would love it. Lots of Cuban artwork, food, music, and dancing. But hanging out with die-hard *cubiches* (say it like this: coo-*bee*-chess) just isn't what I do with my free time, so I always make some excuse not to go.

I place the flyer in my pocket anyway, to take to Mami. It'll make her day.

At 11:00, Andrew pulls his 4Runner into our semicircular driveway. I wonder who paid for the car, him or Daddy. I'm about to thank him and step out, when he jumps out of the car and comes around to open my door. I hope Papi's watching.

"Thank you, sir!"

"*Gracias a usted, señorita,*" he says in a light southern drawl.

"Hey! That was pretty good! *Gracias* for what, though?"

He shuts the door and leads me to our front porch. "For coming out with me. For throwing napkins . . ."

For showing me your cleavage . . .

"For a fun-filled evening," I add.

When we get to the door, I'm all too aware of a presence on the other side of it. Someone of the maternal nature is watching through the peephole. I try to ignore it and focus on Andrew instead. "We did have fun, didn't we? This was kind of unexpected—"

"Unexpected? Gee, thanks. Am I that much of a Frankenstein?"

I imagine Andrew with a big green head, bolts sticking out of his neck, saying things like "Fire . . . bad." What's scarier is the thought that he *could* play a monster on film, with those eyes, those eyes, those eyes . . . *Ay!*

"No, I didn't mean the fun was unexpected, I meant this." I hold up our hands clenched together. "I haven't told you yet, but I'm leaving for Michigan in August, I just broke up with someone, and I promised myself I wouldn't get—"

"Isa?" He smiles, pulling our hands up and moving in closer.

"Hmmm?"

"One day at a time. We just had one date, that's it. It was fun, wasn't it?"

"Yes, it was. I'm sorry I'm obsessing." With my free hand, I tug on my earlobe furiously, but he grabs my fingers and pulls them away with a grin.

Great, he's figured out the effect his eyes have on me, and he's milking it for all it's worth. "It's okay," he says, lowering his eyes for a moment before looking at me again. "I've been obsessing all night over something too."

"*You've* been obsessing?" Funny, he's seemed nothing but confident this entire night. "Over what, pray tell?"

He looks at the peephole. Then his hand reaches up to cover it. He leans in and brings his lips close to mine. "Over this."

I melt into a major-league kiss, soft and warm, but commanding. Robi wishes he could've kissed like this. And then a thought hits me—I won't be keeping my own promise to stay away from guys this summer.

Nope. I'm a goner.

Five

I hardly saw Andrew the day after our date, except when walking by his field, when he'd tip his baseball cap in my direction, but I haven't stopped thinking about the kiss at my front door. It was different, controlled, like he's used to it. Unlike weakling me.

Mom hasn't mentioned my date anymore since that night, maybe by the grace of God or because my dad's last *déjala* did it. Now it's Saturday, and rather than stir up another windstorm with her, I'm home, helping prepare for tomorrow's big feast—our annual Fourth of July barbecue, which the entire family (all forty of us) feels the need to celebrate at our house. We're the only ones with a pool, so hey! Everybody head over to the Díazes'! They'll cook for us! They'll clean after us! They'll serve us beer!

But a Fourth of July barbecue, Cuban-style, is not what you

might think. Burgers and hot dogs? Hell no! What you want is a massive pig, roasted in a hole in the ground. Coleslaw? Corn on the cob? Nope. *Bocaditos, croquetas,* and *chicharrones.* Vanilla Coke? Wrong again. Why drink that crap when you can have an ice-cold Malta Hatuey?

And the two best parts of all this? One, that my parents don't know I invited Andrew, and two, that he's bringing a Key lime pie to rival my mom's.

"Isa, córtame los limones, por favor." Mami hands me the local, small limes for her reigning winner of all pies. I grab a knife and start slicing them in half. Any moment now I'm going to hear the other side of the Key lime story—the Cuban side.

"Did you know . . ." she begins, gently pressing the graham cracker mixture into the pie mold. "That these *limones* were not called *Kee line* in Cuba?"

I don't answer her. I don't answer because she's not really talking to me. She's talking to an invisible interviewer who has approached her for critical information about Cuba's produce.

Under the faucet she washes her hands free of cracker crumbs. It's interesting that she can wave her hands wildly when she talks and still be able to wash them. "You see, in Cuba, these *limones* were not special *Kee line limones,* they were just plain *limones.* We use them for cooking, for marinating . . ."

Sigh. For making *limonada* . . .

"For making *limonada,*" she adds. "They grew everywhere, in everybody's backyards. But here, everybody makes *sush* a big deal about them, like they're so special."

"They are special, Mami. The regular limes here are the big green ones. These are super bitter."

"And that's the other thing. In Cuba, this *Kee line* was not considered a *line*. It was a *limón*."

As fascinating as I really do find this, I keep quiet, or she'll go on about the way things used to be back you-know-where. And if I hear my mom say *Kee line* one more time, I'm going to leave the juicing to her and go watch my brother work on his hair.

At the other end of the house, I hear a blow dryer. Odd, considering the only two women in the house are in the kitchen. And my dad doesn't have hair. So that only leaves Wonder Boy.

Mami reaches past me to open the pantry, stopping momentarily to caress my shoulder. "*¿Eh, Isa?*"

"*¿Sí, Mami?*"

"I saw the *papelito* you put on the refrigerator."

"The Cuba Expo? Yeah, I put it there for you the other night."

"*¿Sí?* I hadn't noticed it. *Gracias por traérmelo.* Maybe you can come with us this time."

"Yeah, maybe. That'd be fun." Don't hold your breath.

A silence falls between us. "*¿Mi vida?*"

"Yes, Mom?"

"*Eh . . . se me olvido decirte que Robi llamó esta mañana.*"

"What?" I blurt, nearly slicing off my finger in the process.

43

"Robi called me this morning? Why didn't you tell me?"

"Because you were sleeping."

"What did he say?" We agreed not to speak for a while, or at least until I called him. First the e-mail, and now this. I said I needed time off, stubborn fool.

"*Nada*." She shrugs.

"*¿Nada?* Robi called to say *nada*? So he just stayed quiet on the line?"

She runs two cans of sweetened condensed milk under the can opener, then pulls the eggs out of a bowl of warm water. "*Mi vida*, he didn't call you. He called me. We talked about *esto, lo otro*. He just wanted to say hi."

This and that. Somehow I find it hard to believe Robi called to discuss this and that without an ulterior motive. He just wanted to see if I was home, picking my nose and thinking of him. And calling my mom, not me? I don't know what he's trying to do, but if he thinks for one minute that'll make a difference in getting back together—

"I told him to come tomorrow," she announces with the crack of an egg.

In my mind I hear a loud metal *pang!* and a scene flashes before me. Of Robi and Andrew, each outfitted with boxing trunks and gloves, dancing around each other, jabbing. Andrew with a split eyebrow. Robi, a bloody nose. Hanging on to the lower rope of the ring from the floor, I'm shouting, "Boys! Boys! Stop it! Please!"

I put my gaping mouth to good use. "Tell me you're kidding."

"*¿Por qué?*" She uses her hand to speak but forgets that she's holding a spatula. Drops of sweetened condensed milk go spattering against the cabinets.

"What do you mean why? Why? Because you have no business inviting Robi here tomorrow!"

"*Ay*, Isa, please. Robi's been coming to our house *para el cuatro de julio hace dos años.*"

"Hello? Earth to Mom? Robi and I broke up! He's come to our barbecue the last two years because we were to-ge-ther. Robi and I are now broken up. Watch . . . " I mercifully put down the knife, then make an open and closed motion with my hands. "Broken up . . . together . . . broken up . . . together. Broken up! Got it?"

My mother gives me that look. The one that suggests *You're being silly, you're overreacting. You're not really broken up with Robi, you're only imagining it.* "Isa, he may not even come. He said he'd try. I only did it to be nice, *hija.* He was nice to you. You can't just *dees-card* someone like that."

You know . . . I've always considered myself a sane person, one who's managed to handle my Cuban nutjob mother with grace, but enough is enough. This last month has completely done her in. Why is she so out-of-whack? What am I going to do? I already invited Andrew!

"Mami," I say calmly, amazing myself, "I know exactly what you're doing. You invited Robi so that I wouldn't even *think* of inviting Andrew."

"Who?"

"My fellow *teasher*?"

"Oh."

"But you're too late. I already did. I invited both him and Susy, so if there's a showdown here tomorrow, you're the one who's going to deal with it, not me, okay? I gotta pee." Total lie; I just have to get out of here. It's that suffocation thing again.

"*Mi vida . . .*"

Mi vida, my ass.

Outside, my father shovels, then wipes his brow. He's taking a moment's rest from digging the pit for tomorrow's *lechón*. His tank undershirt is soaked with sweat, and his hands are covered with dirt. Despite all this, he's digging in nice pants and dress socks. A sight to behold.

"Papi, you have *got* to do something about that woman."

He circles the pit, looking for a new spot to unearth. "What's there to do? *That woman* is fine the way she is."

"And I thought you were the reasonable one."

He laughs in a way I've loved since as long as I can remember—airily, but with a hint of wheezing. "What happened, Isa?"

"She invited Robi to come tomorrow."

"So?"

"So I invited Andrew to come tomorrow too."

He thinks about this for a moment. "So? She didn't know that."

"Dad? She has no business inviting Robi at all! What is she trying to do?" A mosquito bites my ankle, so I slap it to a premature death.

"I'm sure she's not trying to do anything, Isa. What do you want? For her to drop that boy like a hot potato just because you did?"

I cross my arms. Another mosquito whirs a high-pitched battle cry near my ear.

"Didn't you bring Robi around here and ask everybody to accept him as your boyfriend?" He jabs the shovel into the ground and brings up a good chunk of soil. "Now you want us to forget him just like that? She's not doing it to upset you, Isa. It's just that it'll take her a little longer than it took you."

"I don't believe this." I turn and head back to the house. Both the mosquitoes and my dad are killing me.

"*¿Hija?*"

"*¿Padre?*"

"I know it's frustrating, but try to be more patient with your mother. Please?"

There's something in his face. I don't know what it is. Then, a soft look, the one he saves for his girls. Only his girls. I can't possibly say no to him. "I'll try, Papi. For you."

He blows his kiss, then goes back to digging the pit o' death.

What the heck, I'll give it a shot. I'll ask my brother for his two cents on the situation. To locate Stefan, I follow the bass sound of old school Power 96 music.

Din . . . din . . . din-di-ri-din-din . . .

See? He's in his room. Even though he keeps his door

unlocked, I knock. I really don't want to risk seeing him naked, or worse, blow-drying his hair like a girl.

Freestyle's kickin' in the house tonight . . . move your body from left to right . . .

Stefan actually thinks this music is classic. In reality, that electronic voice stopped sounding futuristic in, like, the year I was born. "Stefan?"

A fully clothed, ready-to-hit-the-town Stefan pulls the door open, smiles, and walks back to his mirror. As if this couldn't get worse, he starts singing.

"Excuse me, loser?" His bed is immaculately made, rows of shoes in the closet, bottles of cologne samples lined up on his dresser, all exposing Stefan's organization mania. "Señor Martha Stewart?"

He sways to the beat, which is actually pretty funky if you can get past the silly words.

"Baboon? Uh . . . I know I'm interrupting your important pre-party grooming ritual, but I need some advice. Hel-lo?"

But Stefan's in a semitrance. He hears me, judging from his nod, but his response is more physical than intellectual. If my brother knows anything, it's physical. I *must* get him one of those disco balls for Christmas.

He turns around to demonstrate exactly what I should do about my situation, even though I haven't even told him what it is yet. Party! Dance! He waves his arms in the air, sinks low to the floor, and bites his lower lip. No words necessary. *Just go with the flow,* his hips tell me.

"Both Robi and this guy I went out with are coming tomorrow!" I shout above the boom. "Plus, Mom's all in my business! Do you have any words of wisdom for me, DJ Díaz?"

DJ Díaz doesn't know wisdom. He knows body movement. He boogies over to me, pulls me by the waist, and invites me to dance. The music is unrelenting. Hey, it's actually a pretty good beat.

"To all you freaks, don't stop the rock . . ." I hear the words somehow flow from my mouth, as well as from Stefan's. How the hell did that happen? We're singing! Oh, God, we're both singing! "That's Freestyle speakin' and you know I'm right!"

We bounce. We sway. We sing. This is fun! How did I know those lyrics? Years of old school filtering into my subconscious, that's how. Osmosis through bedroom walls. We bounce and sway some more. My hair's swinging, tickling the back of my arms. We're laughing. Stefan and I, laughing, dancing, like little kids again, practicing for the show we're going to put on for Mami and Papi in the living room.

What did I come in here for? I forgot already. Oh, yeah. My problem. Stefan's not helping, is he? Well, hold up, maybe he is. I mean, my brother may not be the brightest crayon in the box, but he *is* saying something with this. *So you got two boyfriends coming tomorrow? And the problem is?*

Yeah, really. Two guys both coming here for me. A face-off. One will get on Mom's good side. One dares to bring a Key lime pie made by another.

Are these lyrics actually starting to make sense?

There's a party in the house and we'll be rockin' tonight . . .

Six

They arrive in clusters, ruining the Sunday afternoon silence. *Tía* Marta, *Tío* Pepe, Michi, Nereida, *Abuela* Mimi, *Abuelo* Jaime, *Bisabuela* Anita, and all their children, my *primos*—first cousins, second cousins, enough cousins to remind me that the Pill is one of the greatest inventions of all time.

From my room I hear them laughing. And shouting. And cackling, filling the house with jokes, as well as food. Even from across the house, their voices are loud and clear, telling my parents all they've brought. Flans, cookies, *ensaladas de papa y de macarrones, cerveza*, bags of ice, and toys from the dollar store for the little ones.

Someone flips on the stereo. Now Celia Cruz drowns out the other voices. Bubbly, flutey *salsa* music competes with the chatter. I guess there's no point relishing my quiet room anymore. Either I go and greet the crowd, or I wait for my mother to find me and drag me out by the ear.

I go and greet the crowd.

There's my mom's friend Sandra. She sees me and paints a huge circle in the air with her plastic cup of Costco wine. "Sweetie! Congratulations! How does it feel to be a graduate?"

I kiss her cheek and accept a wimpy hug. "Like I'm in limbo. Not in high school, not in college. Yet, anyway. Just working for the summer."

"Oh, that's right. So you're still counseling the little kids out there in the Everglades? That's so sweet."

"It's not counseling, really, it's teaching. Actually I'm just putting my artistic skills to use. You know, good practice while making a few bucks."

"Oh, okay," she says, nodding with a blank smile, probably because she can't think of anything else to ask, even though she's known me my whole life. "That's great, good for you."

Stefan materializes out of nowhere, sticking his face between us, an arm around my shoulders. "And she's dating the camp's PE coach too." He smiles a mischievous grin, then proceeds to splash some beer on my shirt and our plastic-covered sofa. Yes, that's right, a plastic-covered sofa. As I examine the foul play and wipe the couch with a napkin, Stefan escapes unscathed.

"Shut up! I'm not dating anyone, idiot!" I shout. Dork. I use the napkin to blot my shoulder.

Sandra's got her head cocked, eyebrows frozen in the up

position, apparently disappointed that my mother failed to give her the latest scoop. "You're dating someone?" She looks around for Mami and spots her behind me saying hello to the Hewitts from across the street. *"Elena, tú no me dijiste que Isa estaba—"*

"No, Sandra, Isa no está dating anybody."

Should it surprise me that Mami managed to overhear our conversation, exercise the Jedi mind trick, *and* greet the neighbors all at the same time? Now this is skill, people.

Let me just leave Sandra some food for thought. It'll drive her crazy and will arrive at my mother's ears in two minutes flat. "She's right. I wouldn't call it 'dating.'"

While Sandra's still thinking this over, Coach Andrew and Susy enter the living room, with Dad behind them. They're all looking for me, so I lift a hand and excuse myself from Sandra's trap. "See you later. You look great, by the way!"

"Ay, gracias, mi hija." She runs a hand through her hair.

I bounce over to Andrew and Susy. "Hey there."

"Hey." Susy and I exchange air smooches. I notice her surveying me out of the corner of her eye as I brush cheeks with Andrew. "So, what's up?" she asks, scanning the party crowd. "Is Patty here yet?"

"She might be outside."

"I'll go check." She struts off to find the gossip queen of our family.

"Dad," I say, pulling him back before he has the chance to walk away. "You met Andrew?"

"Yes." Dad pats Andrew on the back, like he's found a new

protégé. "A business major. Good, good." Then he goes out-side to check the death pit and see how the *lechón* is doing. We follow him onto the patio.

"Nice house," Andrew says. There's a very subtle hush, and I can feel forty pairs of eyes on us. I can just imagine everyone's questions now. *Who's that guy? Where's Robi? Is that Isa's new beau? ¿Quién coño es ese tipo?*

Before I can even say thanks, hello, how you doin', want a *croqueta?*, Stefan presses a cold bottle of Corona to my neck, and I squeal, "You jerk!" This is to attract the attention of anyone who may not already be noticing Andrew and me, such as the babies, dragonflies, and people across the canal.

Stefan thinks this is extremely funny and a clever way of getting me to introduce Andrew to him. "Yo, bro, what's up? I'm her brother." He extends a hand to my guest.

"Stefan," I tell Andrew. "'Brother' isn't his real name."

Andrew takes his hand, and they shake like buddies. "Andrew."

"Like the hurricane."

"Exactly."

"Actually he *is* a Hurricane," I clarify.

Apparently, from the way he's staring at me, like his seventeen-year-old sister shouldn't be calling a guy she's only gone out with once a hurricane, Stefan still doesn't get what I mean.

I shake my head. "A UM Hurricane, fool!"

"Oh!" Stefan tilts his head back, hand on his hip, other hand on his beer. "So you play football? That's cool."

Jesus. He's hopeless.

Andrew tries helping Stefan out. "No, bro. I just go to school there."

"Oh."

"Yeah, as in study?" I say. "As in he does something with his life besides scope the beach for *sucias*?"

"For what?" Andrew asks.

"'Hos,'" I explain.

"*Coño*, Isa, I do not look for *sucias*. *¿Qué te pasa? ¿Tu 'tá nerviosa porque Fulanito 'tá aquí?*"

I hate when he does this. It's so rude of him to tell me things in Spanish when someone else around doesn't understand him. It's like abusing a superhuman power.

Andrew clears his throat. "There's nothing wrong with her. I really don't think she's nervous 'cause of me, dude."

Unbelievable. He understood. This is great! Go, Andrew!

"Oh, you speak Spanish?" Stefan acts happy about this. "That's awesome, bro! So . . . *mira, allí 'tá la cerveza*," he rattles off at rapid fire. "*Seguro que la vas a encontrar rapidito porque tienes un olor a cerveza encima de madre.*"

Andrew squints, turns his ear to Stefan. "Dude, I only know a little bit, so you gotta talk slower than that."

"Oh, okay." Stefan appears pleased. "I said, help yourself to a beer." He winks and walks off, whispering, "*Está más feo qu'el carajo.*"

Asshole. Thank God Andrew missed that one. He wouldn't have appreciated my brother saying that he reeks of beer and is uglier than hell. What upsets me is that Stefan didn't know for sure that Andrew wouldn't understand him, so he just took a risk in getting his ass kicked.

But hold up . . . is Stefan serious? Does Andrew really reek? I've been aware of something, but I thought it was the spill on my shirt. Now I really want to lean in and check for myself, but that would be too weird.

Instead, we walk to the patio table and hang out for a while, during which time I don't notice any funny smells. I point out the various characters in my family, including Evelina, my dad's flamboyant aunt, who currently entertains a thirty-year-old banker in her bedroom, despite her sixty-two years.

"Don't ask," I say. "She's been serving the male public since her husband died nine years ago." I remember Evelina changing practically overnight, like she was just waiting for the old guy to drop dead so she could cut loose.

Evelina notices us eyeing her and waves happily. We smile and wave back.

"She looks good for sixty-two," Andrew says, side-glancing me for a reaction.

"Ha, ha." He better be kidding.

Susy comes back with Patty, who drapes an arm around my shoulders. Leaning her head against mine, Patty whispers, "He's hot, Isa! Where'd you get him?"

I ignore her. "Andrew, this is my cousin Patty."

"Hey, nice to meet you." He smiles.

A breath of air escapes her that sort of sounds like hi. She and Susy then exchange funny looks, like they're agreeing on

Andrew's hotness. I wonder if the other girls here think the same of him.

Susy and Patty begin their commentary on the barbecue fashion faux pas while strolling around the patio. I look at Andrew and cross my arms. "Hey, where's that pie you promised me?"

"Ah, the best dessert on Earth? I dropped it off on your kitchen counter. We'll test it later."

"Yes, and we'll find out who rules, baby!"

My aunt Clarita whizzes by quickly, smiling politely, but announcing, *"Escóndete, que ahí llegó el rey de España."*

"You're kidding," I say. Dammit. Robi's here.

"What did she just say?" Andrew asks, squinting. "About the king of Spain?"

"That my ex-boyfriend's arrived to join the fun." I roll my eyes. So embarrassing. "Sorry. He's not a jerk or anything. Probably won't even bother us."

His eyes open wide. "Really? So, what is he, a part of the family?"

"Some people think so. I haven't seen him in a month, though. I have no idea why he's here."

Speaking of which, I haven't seen my mother in a while either. Haven't even introduced Andrew to her. I would've, but after I left her in the kitchen last night, we haven't really spoken. She's been so busy ignoring me and Coach, I figure she's taking Robi's side. Well, that's just fine.

When Robi finally appears at the sliding glass doors, wearing a dark blue shirt with giant white stars on it and holding a paper plate, my stomach begins to ache. It's only been a month, but he looks different. He cut his hair. He's skinnier or something. Some people greet him heartily, some pretend not to see him, and some just smile faintly as he walks by. Susy says hello to him. He gives her a friendly kiss, then looks around nervously.

"Is that him?" Andrew asks. From across the yard, I see Susy making a face at me, behind Robi's back, like she thinks this situation is highly amusing.

"Yep." I try not to look at her or Robi. Don't want him thinking I miss him. Don't want the rest of the nosy clan to think the same either.

Robi's never been the shy type, so it wouldn't surprise me if he came over. In fact, that's exactly what he seems to be doing, accompanied by Stefan. Robi just *has* to show everyone he has no bad feelings toward me and can handle this situation like a man. As he makes his way over, greeting a handful of my folks, I catch him looking at me then looking away. Finally he makes it to my corner of the yard.

"Hey, Isa," he says, shy smile at his lips. He looks at Andrew for a moment.

"Hey, Robi." I tug once at my earlobe, and Andrew pulls my hand away.

Robi glares at him for a moment. Then he bends down to kiss my cheek, which feels really weird after two years of lip-locking, and I notice what's on his plate. A slice of Key lime pie. And it's green. Major, and I do mean major, no-no! It must be Andrew's mom's. Mami would never put food coloring in the naturally yellow filling. Sacrilege!

Andrew offers his hand to Robi, who accepts it with the most serious attitude he can manage. After Robi starts to tell Stefan about a movie he saw last night, Andrew notices his mom's pie and elbows me lightly. "See?" he says with a wicked smile. "Your mama's going down."

"Loser," I tease back.

Behind Robi, Mami comes rounding the pool, a nervous smile on her face. She reaches us and puts one hand on Robi's shoulder, another on Baboon's. *"¿Isa, viste quién está aquí?"*

"No, Mami, I'm blind. Who's here?"

Robi laughs.

Mom doesn't. In fact, she completely ignores the remark, while eyeing Andrew at the same time. Andrew reaches up and takes her hand. *"Mucho gusto, Señora Díaz. Yo soy Andrew."*

Awesome! His accent's not that bad. Go Andrew, go Andrew!

Robi then turns to my mother, and, right there in front of us, inserts his foot as far back into his mouth as possible. "Elena, you make the best, most awesome Key lime pie." He takes a huge forkful and downs it in a second flat.

Ay, ay, ay! I do *not* believe this. From the look on Mom's face, she doesn't either. She's staring at Robi, tongue tucked into her cheek, waiting for a lightbulb to turn on inside his brainless head. When it doesn't, she turns without a word and walks away. Stefan grips Robi's shoulder in sympathy and takes off too.

Robi stands there with me and Andrew, trying to figure out what just happened.

"Robi," I say, "my mom doesn't put green food coloring in her pie. It's not traditional, remember?"

"Oh." He looks down at his hand, as if he was holding a plateful of crap.

Hand over my face, I shake my head. "I can't believe you just dissed my mom! And straight to her face, too! You better go kiss and make up. She's the president of your fan club, after all."

Frazzled, Robi turns around and starts talking to my uncle Tony and his brother-in-law's former girlfriend's roommate. Exactly.

Andrew leans his head on my shoulder and releases a quiet laugh. "Oh, my, God. Your ex just failed the freakin' taste test!" He shudders from the hilarity of it all. I lean my head on his and laugh too. Poor Robi, he should've just quit while he was ahead. That's what he gets for coming here.

From across the yard, I see Papi, arm around Mom's shoulder, leaning down in his usual consoling position. Great, she's wounded.

"I'll be right back. You'll be okay?" I ask Andrew. He nods, still grinning from ear to ear. I have to find out what's wrong with Mami. As I step away, I see I'll have to squeeze between Uncle Tony and Robi in order to get by. Something's gonna have to rub against him. Boobs or butt?

But then, it happens—the one thing we can honestly say has never happened at a Díaz Fourth of July barbecue.

Robi steps back to let me through, and that's when his sneaker goes *squeak*! Everyone near us gasps in horror, and the rest seems to happen very slowly. He slips off the ground, Key lime pie flying, napkin fluttering, arms waving, plate flipping, shirt billowing . . . all crashing into the deep end of the pool with a loud, sickening *splash*!

And, of course, all forty pairs of eyes fall on me.

Seven

I didn't do it. But there was no convincing Robi of that, so he accepted a change of clothes and went home. The rest of the day sucked after that. Everybody scarfed down Mami's Key lime pie but me. Andrew's mom's was okay. Coach said he'd done enough damage and would call me later.

But I still haven't heard from him, and it's 9:30 at night. So I open Outlook and find another e-mail from Robi.

From: Roberto Puertas
To: Isa Díaz
Subject: Nice party, Isa

Thanks for the push. Just what I needed after seeing you with that guy. Your brother told me you work with him. Maybe it's not such a good idea to be the youngest teacher at that camp, huh? Whatever, not like it's any of my business anymore. Have a nice summer.

Robi

Exactly what does he mean by "not such a good idea"? That Susy and Andrew are too old to be my friends? What would he rather I do, hang out with high school freshmen? Oh yes, that would keep me safely away from harm, now wouldn't it. Why can't he just leave me alone for a while like I asked?

As I'm logging off, Mom comes into my room to drop off a laundry basket. She leans on the doorframe and picks at her nails. "*¿Isa, qué pasó hoy?*"

I swivel around in my desk chair. "What do you mean?"

"Today. What happened? Did you push Robi, *mi hija?*"

Oh, Lord. "You're not serious. You seriously think I would push Robi in the pool, Mami?"

Of course, she answers with a question. "Why are you doing this to him, Isa?"

"Doing what? I'm not doing anything! It's time for me to move on, that's all. If you love Robi so much, rent my room out to him once I'm gone! Jeez."

Uh-oh, she's going to snap at me, here it comes . . .

She doesn't. She just stands there, straightening the stack of books on my dresser. "*¿Mi hija, qué te pasa últimamente?*"

I don't believe this. "Mami, nothing is wrong with me lately. You're the one who's been acting all strange, getting into my business more than usual, and going off crying when Robi says he likes someone else's Key lime pie. What's with that?"

"*Isa, no sabes lo que estás hablando.*"

"Oh, no? Well, maybe if you talked to me more, I would know what I'm talking about. But instead, you just argue, pick fights, and invite my ex-boyfriend over without asking me!"

"Ah, so now he's the ex-boyfrrrien, *cuando hace dos años, no había ni día ni noche sin Robi?*"

When did I ever say the world revolved around Robi? "Yes, Mom, it happens, okay? People go their separate ways. I'm sorry you're having such a hard time with it."

She's quiet again, probably shocked at hearing me talk this way, I think. She would expect this from Carmen but not from me. "*¿Quién era ese niño que vino?*"

"I tried telling you, but you didn't want to hear it. His name's Andrew, like he told you. He's the guy I had coffee with. He's nice; I like him. So I invited him over. What's the big deal?"

"How old is he?"

I don't even know. That should probably be the first question to ask anybody on a date, but we had such a good time, it never occurred to me. "I'm not sure, Mom. I guess around twenty."

I can tell she's trying real hard to stay out of my business, but she can't. Number one, because she's a mom, and number two, because she's a Cuban mom. If she doesn't pester me to death about my life, they just might revoke her Cuban Mother License to Drive Daughters Away.

"*Isa, no es buena idea.* Listen to me . . . he's older than you, *mi vida*, he's in college, things are different for him. *¿Tú me entiendes?*"

"No, I don't understand. What are you saying? That because he's older, I can't handle him? Do I not use my best judgment? Did you not teach me about life properly?"

Why is she staring at me? She's wondering if I've been talking to Carmen. Damn, I really sounded like Carmen just now, didn't I? She has to know what's coming next.

"Don't you trust me?" I ask for the four hundredth time in my life.

She sighs. "*No es eso, hija.*"

"Well, if that's not it, then what is it?"

She doesn't answer. Again. Just spaces out. "*No sé,*" she says finally. "*Hablamos mañana,* I'm tired."

And she leaves. Just like that. Really weird.

I know that Mom freaked out the summer before Carmen left for college too, so this is probably the same thing. She's scared because I'm leaving and doesn't know how to say it, so she's looking for other reasons to argue. Weird way of saying I love you, please don't leave, isn't it?

Monday is a day off, but Andrew ends up calling late at night. My parents are outside talking, which is good, so I don't have to explain such a late phone call.

"Hey, there!" Cheery, cheery.

"Hi, Coach. How are you?"

"Good. Sorry I didn't call last night. I went fishing with

Iggy and his dad, and we got back early this morning. Then I slept pretty much all day. Killer hangover."

Attractive thought. Andrew sleeping off a buzz, like Stefan does sometimes, when Mom thinks he's coming down with something. I guess that's college life for you. I'll be seeing it soon enough, so it's good that I get a preview now. "That's okay. You don't have to explain."

Why do I care that he didn't call sooner? He's not my boyfriend or anything. "I thought maybe you got scared, after watching me throw my ex into the pool."

"Oh, that? Nah. That was me actually. I used my super mental powers to trip him, and down he went."

I crack up, but suddenly feel stupid for doing so. "Andrew?" I ask, my laughter lulling. "You know, I know I haven't asked you this, but how old are you?"

He chuckles softly. "Hmmm, don't know. My real parents left me on someone's doorstep when I was just a baby, so no one knows for sure."

I giggle some more. By now he probably thinks I'm a fool who laughs at anything, but this *is* nice for a change. Robi never made me laugh. It was always me amusing him.

"Seriously, how old do you think I am?" he asks.

"Um, twenty? Twenty-one?"

"Warm."

Okay. "Nineteen?" If he graduated at seventeen like I did, I guess he could be starting his third year of coursework and be nineteen.

He laughs. "Nope. Cold."

Uh-oh. I tug on my earlobe. "How old are you then?"

He lets out a heavy sigh. "Twenty-three, *señorita*."

I'm sorry, but it sounded like he said TWENTY-THREE? What?! No way! That's older than Stefan! The oldest person I ever kissed was Robi! I could've sworn Andrew was no more than twenty. But twenty-three? That's like . . . like . . . out of my league. Awesome!

Awesome? Isa! Does he even know how old you are?

"Hello?" His voice seems deeper to me now for some reason. "Anybody there?"

"Yeah, I'm here," I breathe. "Sorry, I just—" My stomach's working those butterflies again. "But you said you were a junior."

"I am. After my first year my grades weren't all that, too much partying, I guess. So my parents made me go home and work for the money I'd lost them. UM's expensive, you know."

"I know." Silence.

"Is something wrong?" He sounds way older now. You know, maybe I'm liking this age thing.

"No, it's just that . . . well, Andrew, how old do you think *I* am?"

"You just graduated high school, right? So . . . eighteen?"

Oh, brother. Here we go. I hope I'm not dropping a bomb here. "Seventeen actually."

"Oh."

"But my birthday's next month, August twelfth. Look, it doesn't bother me, if it doesn't bother you. I mean, we can still go out again if you want."

I hate these painful silences. What's he thinking? Great, I bet now he doesn't want to go out again. *Let's just stay happy coworkers, eh?* Maybe he'll move on to Susy now. But that kiss! So incredible. I definitely want more.

His voice is lower now, sexy. "Are you asking me out?" I can just see that wide smile of his. Oh, Jesus.

"I guess I am." And using my notes on classic Susy flirting, I add, "Come by my room tomorrow for another art demonstration."

"Hmmm," he muses softly. "I'll be there after the bell, *señorita*."

Eight

Remember Iggy's flying niece? Well, Chicken-Chickee's real name is Daisy. She's in my 3:30 class. Pretty good with the oil pastels actually. In the five minutes I've been working with her, the little chatterbox has told me all about *Tío* Iggy, the pretty girl he used to bring to her house, and the older brother she wished she had.

"But I have a fake brother," she announces.

"Really?" I gotta wrap this up. The kids are getting antsy, and it's almost 4:30. "Look, blend these two and you get the color of the morning sun. See?"

"Oh, cool, Miss Díaz. Well, my fake brother? His name's Andy. Maybe you know him because he's a teacher here too."

"You mean Coach Andrew?" Her fake brother. That's so cute. "Yeah, I've met him, Daisy. He's real nice."

"I know. But *Tío* Iggy got mad at him and now they don't

live together anymore."

Mad at him? "Why did Iggy get mad at him?" I ask.

She shrugs. "I don't know."

"But they're still friends, right?" They must be. They went fishing together last weekend.

"I think so. But Andy? He throws me in the air higher than my dad or my *tío*."

Hmmm, they got into a fight? Over what? Probably over who gets the shag pad to themselves on which night and all that. Whatever. I'll ask more tomorrow. Only two minutes to the bell, then Andrew's coming. "Yeah, he looks like he could make you fly," I tell her, and she holds up her pattern for me to behold. "Beautiful! Let's put it up."

It's 4:30 on the dot. I take the kids out in a single file, and they board the buses in time to escape the rain. When I get back to my room, I pretend to be really busy shelving the Cray-Pas. Two minutes later Coach walks in. He leans his equipment bag against the wall.

He closes the door most of the way and tips his baseball cap. "*Hola*. How was your day?" He steps slowly, careful not to knock down the chairs up on the little tables.

"Long." This is totally true. I've been dying to see him today, dying to know if he'll act the same with me, wondering if we'll kiss again. I pull out my easel from the closet, the one with my painting.

"Same here," he says, watching me prepare brushes, cloth, mineral spirits. He then sits on a low countertop next

69

to me. "You're going to work on that some more, I see?"

"Yes, I want to add a beach. This girl's sitting on the sand, looking out, but I still don't know what she wants or what she's thinking. I guess no one'll ever really know."

"Kind of like the Mona Lisa."

"Exactly. Like the Mona Lisa." I smile, happy that he recognizes the mystery behind da Vinci's masterpiece. Most people my age wouldn't know anything about the Mona Lisa.

I focus on my canvas and begin blending the oils on my palette, trying to get the right tone for the sand to complement the dark clouds. Scraping off my brush, I start dabbing the paint onto the canvas. Andrew watches without a word. The real storm clouds outside start rumbling, announcing their daily visit. That's summer in the Everglades for you. And they call this the Sunshine State.

I work the paint in quickly, because I want to finish this section before I leave today. It feels a little strange to have an audience. I almost never paint with someone watching. This is my quiet time. I'm usually alone. Andrew barely moves or breathes. Outside I hear the sound of some kids squealing, as the rain starts to come down. A sweet smell wafts into the room. Perfect rain.

Andrew, maybe sensing my love of stormy afternoons, stands up and moves behind me to get cozier. He leans his chin on my shoulder for a better view. "Is this bothering you? Just tell me."

"No, it's not," I hear myself say kind of quickly. It probably *should* bother me . . . I mean, I'm working here . . . but it doesn't. Not in the slightest. It feels nice to have someone genuinely admiring my one real talent.

"Just tell me if I start bugging you."

He reaches around my waist and links his hands, like we're slow-dancing to the sound of the rain. My stomach starts fluttering again. That's practically zero butterflies in the last two years, and now a whole multitude has visited me these last few weeks. Why am I going so crazy over him?

Weakling. You're a weakling, Isa.

I probably shouldn't be able to concentrate on this painting with him holding me like this, yet I can. His being here helps me, as I work the oils. The storm outside now pounds the roof. Maybe I should always have him around. Maybe Andrew's my muse.

He turns his face toward me, getting a close look as I paint. He's enjoying this, watching me work—the girl, this beach, these clouds, listening to the downpour outside and the sound of my breathing. And then, oh God, the final touch . . . he moves his mouth to my neck and kisses me softly. Once. His mouth lingers there, totally and completely teasing me.

Okay, *now* I can't concentrate.

He pulls me closer. I can feel his every contour. *Every* contour. My grip on the paintbrush slips. My hands are sweating. And then, I realize I'm swooning again, like the first time he came in here. The room is sort of swirling, not completely dizzying, but enough for me to forget where I am for a second. My eyes close.

Exactly what kind of special power does he have to make me feel like this? It's not right. I'm leaving soon; we shouldn't be doing this. I have to tell him.

"Andrew?"

Just the rain answers me, and I really don't feel like interrupting again. Maybe I should listen to my brother's wisdom. *Go with the flow. Don't think, Isa, go with the way things feel.*

"Just tell me to stop, and I will," he whispers into my neck, my cheek, kissing my earlobe. He's so sweet, so damn sweet.

God, this isn't fair! How can I think clearly when he's doing this? My other hand reaches up to his neck, instinctively pulling him closer to me. And before I can think or do anything else, I hear a wooden tap on the floor. My paintbrush, right out of my hand.

This is crazy.

Man. The word comes out of nowhere. Barely noticeable. *Andrew's not a boy, Isa. He's a man. He expects more.* I know I said I could handle this situation, but with every press of his body against me, with every kiss, I realize this won't end here. It won't even end at second or third base. Maybe not today, but sometime before summer's up, Andrew Corbin will score a home run at Isa Field.

Jeez, I am *so* not in control of this situation! But I don't care. It feels incredible. I always had to be in control with Robi. Andrew makes me want to relax and not think. Just feel. Suddenly I turn around and give in to his kiss, his arms, full force, and only then do I feel Andrew slightly lose control as he leans back against the counter.

Then, the craziest thought enters my head. *Stay, don't go. Michigan's not that great, anyway.*

Before I can reply to my evil inner thought, we hear a loud voice outside the classroom door. It's Susy, shouting "See you tomorrow" to someone down the hall. She pushes my door open, and Andrew lets go of me. He crosses his arms quickly, trying to look like we were just discussing world peace.

But she sees us and stops cold. "Oh . . . hey . . . I was just coming to tell you, Isabel . . . there's an art contest. Forget it, I'll tell you later." She eyes Andrew. There's a certain look on her face. Hurt? Why? He's never so much as looked her way. Just because she's got it for him? Well, hell, Susy's got it for anybody!

I straighten my shirt. "No, wait, what contest, Suse?"

"Stop by the main house before you leave. It's on the bulletin board. There's a *prize*," she enunciates, like I don't need any more prizes with Andrew here.

"Thanks. I'll take a look."

She backs out of the room, glancing at Andrew again before closing the door.

I feel bad, but don't know why. I don't have to feel bad about anything. I know Susy thinks Andrew's hot, but so what? Everyone thinks Andrew's hot.

"What was that all about?" he asks with a heavy sigh.

"I don't know. She's jealous or something." I pick the paintbrush off the floor and place it in the cup. "She *did* kind of hint she liked you the first day of camp."

"Well, I guess I didn't notice, did I?" He smiles.

73

"Whatever. She'll get over it."

Andrew reaches over and runs his fingers through my bangs, letting the chunks of hair fall slowly to my face. "I gotta go."

"I know. Me too."

"Isa? I just want to tell you that I'm really into you." His intense eyes transform into a puppy dog look. "In case you're wondering what's going on here." He takes my hand and swings it lightly.

"Okay," I say brilliantly. Like he even has to say that. His constant attention sort of speaks for itself.

"Seriously. You're talented. I mean, look at this," he says, gesturing at my painting, "*and* you're gorgeous, *and* you're funny. It never ends." He resumes his hold on my waist and presses his forehead against mine. "I'd be crazy not to want to go out with you again."

Right. And I should say something, rather than stand here like a complete wanker. "It doesn't bother me, if it doesn't bother you. I mean, the whole age thing."

"It doesn't bother me at all. I wasn't even thinking about it."

And we kiss again, for quite a while. Only this time, I'm sure it won't be the last.

Nine

"So what's going on with you guys?" Susy asks me at lunch two days later.

She avoids my eyes, examining her sandwich instead.

"What do you mean?" The make-out session with Coach, duh.

"What do you mean *what do I mean*? You and Andrew. Are you guys going out? Or was that a one-shot deal you were starting the other day?"

One-shot deal? No, that's you, sister. "Why are you asking like that? What are you, mad? Look, I can't help it if he likes me." Okay, I just flipped my palm up, like my mother does.

It's quiet as she thinks about this. "Yes, but you never said you were interested in him."

"I know I didn't, because I wasn't. But then I got to know him, and now I like him." My volume gets a bit loud, and a couple people look over from the other table.

"Shh." Susy leans in, glancing up at my face. "Look, just take it easy with him. He's a lot older than you are."

"And?" She's never cared this much about me before, but now she gets all sisterly? "He's twenty-three, not fifty."

"Doesn't matter. His agenda is different than yours."

"And how do you know what his agenda is?" I ask, looking her straight in the eye. "Or mine for that matter? What if my agenda includes seeing Andrew as much as I please?"

She leans back again, getting comfortable in her chair. "Oh, that's right. You did say, 'No, I'm not going to meet anyone this summer, I want a clean slate, I'm leaving for Michigan,' blah, blah, blah."

"So? I didn't expect to meet someone new. It just happened."

"Well, I'm just looking out for you. I remember Iggy saying his roommate was always drunk. He was probably talking about Andrew," she says, letting it sink in for a moment before taking a sip of her Coke.

Nice! So now she's trying to make him an alcoholic so I won't go out with him? She's that desperate? Or does she think there's no one to look out for me, since my sister's not around and everything?

"Thanks, but I don't need another mom. I already have the mother of all mothers, plus Carmen." This is really starting to piss me off. It's not like she wrote her name on his forehead with a Sharpie or anything.

"Suit yourself." She stands and scoops up her brown bag,

plastic bag, and soda can. She dumps them into the garbage, then leaves the teachers' lounge.

Like I need this from her. I thought Susy was beyond jealousy, with that careless attitude of hers, but I guess not. Interesting, the defense mechanisms people will put up sometimes. I honestly didn't think she liked him that badly. Well, sorry, girlfriend, that's life. Deal with it.

I have five minutes before picking up the kids from the cafeteria, so I go by the main house. Between Susy's intrusion and Andrew's tongue the other day, I forgot to check out the art contest she mentioned. Better take a look. I'll need all the extra bucks I can get before leaving for college.

On the bulletin board I spot the bright blue paper. Well, what do you know? The contest is for Cuba Expo, and the deadline is July 29. Today's the 8th. Wouldn't that be something? Actually going to the stupid thing this year for a contest, not at my mom's insistence? The first prize is only $100, though, which sucks. And guess what? My painting isn't about anything Cuban. So there goes that.

On my way home it starts again. The stupid rain. One day, fine, two days, okay. Now it's rained, like, four days in a row, and I can't see a damned thing in front of me. Then you have the people driving out from the city, who don't remember to turn on their lights when going down Tamiami Trail. And then they wonder why oncoming cars don't see them when they pass. My windshield wipers are already swishing on high.

What do I do about Susy? Nothing, I guess. She'll have to get over it. What about Andrew? I really like him, but I hope I'm not falling for him. *That* would only make things worse. What have I gotten into? It's like I've fallen into a trap, but the trap is a wonderful green land with lots of bubbling brooks, mango trees, and sunflowers. Okay, scratch the sunflowers. They make me sneeze.

I get to 147th Avenue with no problems. Except, the driver of an eighteen-wheeler next to me is either blind or extremely high, because suddenly he moves right into my lane, practically scraping my sideview mirror.

"God damn!" I swerve off the road to avoid getting crushed. My truck drops off the soft shoulder and into a shallow ditch, just barely missing one of those concrete barricades. The stupid truck continues on like nothing happened!

"*¡Me cago en tu madre! ¡Hijo de puta!*"

Fabulous, this is just the best day ever. This is exactly why I always pester Mom for my own cell phone—in case of emergencies. But no, she said, I would only use it to talk to friends at inappropriate times, like school, or work, or God forbid, in an actual emergency! Now I'll have to wait here for the rain to stop so I can walk to Publix on 137th Avenue to use the phone.

"This sucks!" I don't think there's any damage, but still, my hands are shaking and my stomach hurts. Now Mami will find out what happened and get on my case even more. As it is, she's about to beg me to stay at the end of the summer, I just know it. And there's no way I'm staying in Miami.

You know the best part about this city? The way the traffic whooshes by, ignoring the truck sitting here in the rain, in a ditch, with its hazards on. *Oh, would you look at that, a driver in need of assistance. I sure hope someone comes to help her soon. Bye-bye!* And there they go. Thanks a lot, people!

Oh wait, someone's here. I see the lights bounce up behind me, and the car makes its way over the bumpy ground. In the rearview mirror I see it's a white 4Runner. Ha, Andrew. Now why does that not surprise me?

A bright orange–sheathed body gets out of the car and jogs over to my passenger side. I click the door open.

He gets in, pulling back the hood of his Hurricanes poncho, water droplets sliding and soaking into the seats. "Need help, ma'am?"

Great rescue! Way better than AAA.

"Hey!" Yes, I know . . . clever reply.

"Good thing there's only one road out of camp."

"Yeah, and another good thing that you left after I did, or you wouldn't have seen me. Can you believe what happened?" I recount the story of the rain, the eighteen-wheeler, and how happy I am to have plummeted into a shallow area and not off any one of Miami's dozens of bridges.

"Wow, what an idiot. He was probably drunk off his ass."

"No kidding. How the hell am I going to get out of here?"

"You'll need a tow truck," he says, looking back at his car. "I have my phone. Be right back."

He runs out to retrieve his cell. I feel so stupid, a damsel in distress. As I'm waiting for him to come back, I see another party has arrived. Florida Highway Patrol, blue lights circling silently. Great. Girl gets run off the road, sits in a ditch like a dork, while men save her helpless butt.

She gets out. A woman officer. Why did I assume it would be a guy? She knocks on Andrew's window, he lowers it, and I see them talking. He points, he smiles. She looks around, she smiles. A moment later Andrew is running back this way.

He rushes in and slams the door. "Okay, I called a tow truck. She's gonna wait with us until they get here. See? You'll be okay, missy."

"I can't believe this crap. Thanks, Coach."

"No problem, *señorita*." He wipes rain off his face and leans in to give me a kiss. His skin smells like grass, sun, and rain all mixed together. Intoxicating. I hope the tow truck takes its time. I could stay here all day with Andrew.

By 6:30, the sky has cleared, like the rain never happened, and my father's car sits in the driveway. Mami isn't back yet from wherever, which is really weird. Good. I'd hate for her to worry about me any more than she already does, especially with Andrew following me home. Dad opens the door before I can even use my keys.

"*¿Ey? ¿Y qué?*"

"Hey, Dad. Did you get my message?"

"I haven't checked. *¿Por qué?*"

"Because I kinda had an accident, but I'm fine." I kiss his

cheek and drop my stuff on the sofa. Andrew follows me in and shakes Dad's hand.

My dad barely notices the exchange, worry all over his face. "An accident? *¿Hija, qué pasó?*"

"Nothing, an eighteen-wheeler drove me off the road, and I couldn't get out of a ditch. Andrew found me. A tow truck pulled me out. Just a scratch on the Chevy."

Dad listens, glancing at Andrew appreciatively.

I sit on the sofa. "Where's Mom?"

"Eh, she had a checkup in the afternoon. *Probablemente está sentada en tráfico. Ese Kendall está de madre.*" He looks at Andrew again, this time to clarify in English. "She's probably sitting in—"

"Kendall traffic," Andrew interrupts. "I got it."

Dad smiles. "Oh, that's good. Very good." He kneads the back of my neck, a pat on the back for reeling in a good one. My dad has always appreciated my judgment of anything, even guys. So *not* typical of Cuban dads. One reason why I love him.

Andrew looks around. "Mind if I use your bathroom?"

I point toward the bedrooms. "Right around the corner, next to the giant picture of me in the cream puff dress."

He walks off, and a moment later I hear him laughing down the hall.

My dad sinks onto the couch next to me, placing a hand on my knee. "*Isa, no le digas nada a tu mamá de lo que pasó.*"

Don't tell my mom anything? "*¿Por qué?*"

"*Porque sí.* She worries enough about everything without

knowing that you're out there falling off roads. She's *estressed* for anything." I love the way my dad says stressed. Otherwise, his English is pretty darn near perfect.

"So I sent her to see Dr. Hernández," he adds.

Any little thing wrong with anyone, and my dad suggests a visit to Dr. Hernández, family friend and physician. "Why, do you think he'll be able to figure her out? It's more here"— I point to my head—"than anything. That'll take more than a tongue depressor down her throat, *tú no crees?*"

"*Chica, deja a tu pobre madre ya.*"

"Fine, I'll get off her case for a while. I'm only on it because she doesn't leave me alone. She treats me like a baby, Dad. Sometimes I wish Carmen were here to share in Mami's insanity."

"Oh, and Robi called you," he adds.

I roll my eyes. Robi again? Why can't he let me be? If I call him back, it'll do more harm than good.

Andrew reappears, rubbing his hands together. He touches my arm lightly. "All right, I guess I'll be going now."

"'K."

"*Hasta luego, mi hijo,*" Dad says.

"*Adiós, señor.*" Andrew nods. Most Cubans don't really say *adiós*, but "see you later." Still, at least he tries.

We walk to the front door. "Thanks for rescuing me." *Prince Andrew.*

"Hey, no problem. Call me later?"

"Okay."

Another kiss. A quick good-bye on the lips. *Call me later?*

Man, Andrew and I have been talking every day this week. Do I mind? Hell no. He makes me swoon, remember? That alone means something. There has to be something wrong with him. Nobody's that perfect.

I watch as he pulls out of my driveway, wet tires squeaking against the sidewalk. Then, in the rosy light of the waning sun, he takes off on his white horse. 4Runner, I mean.

Ten

Friday night, we ate in the Grove. It felt different to be on a date with someone who ordered two pints of Sam Adams. I wouldn't necessarily call Andrew a drunk, though. I can't believe Susy actually tried that one on me. Anyway. After tipping the belly dancer and splitting a skyscraping dessert, we strolled Cocowalk. He bought me the cutest bracelet with brown stones and beads.

When we got back to my house, nobody was home, so we kissed in his car for, like, half an hour. I had to force myself to say good night or I honestly don't know what would've happened. Believe me, it wasn't easy.

Last night, I didn't see him. He went fishing with Iggy's family again. He said he'd bring us dolphinfish today if they caught any, but it's already 2:00. Last Monday he called late. Therefore, I seriously doubt we'll see any fresh fish today.

Before accompanying Mami to Sedano's, I check my e-mail and find two new messages, one from Robi (how've you been please call me, *aargh!*) and one from Carmen. I spin the bracelet Andrew gave me over my wrist as I read the one from my sister:

From: C. Díaz-Sanders
To: Isabelita
Subject: Patience pays

Hi, baby girl. Dad says you've been losing it with Mami. Take it easy, sweetie. You know how she is . . . her bark is worse than her bite. Hang in there for another four weeks, and try to make your summer with her as pleasant as possible. You may feel exasperated now, but you'll miss her later, believe me. How are things with Andrew, is it? Be careful, sis. Send Stefan a kiss for me, okay?

Love you,
Carmen

Dad said that? Why? Since when does he need help from my sister in talking to me? Mom's the one who looks for confrontation, not the other way around. I can be patient with the endless talk of Fidel the Devil, but when she starts inviting Robi over at her own discretion? That's a different story.

"Isabelita!" Mami barks from the foyer.

"*¡Ya voy!*" I pull off the bracelet and tuck it into my night table drawer. What's the point in her seeing it? It would only launch a discussion that's better left alone.

"*Vámonos,*" she says when I emerge from my room and find her with reddish eyes, purse slung over her shoulder, ready to go food shopping.

What is *that* all about? "*¿Mami, qué pasa?*" I look intently at her eyes.

"*Nada, hija, los lentes de mierda estos me tienen cansada. Es hora de cambiarlos.*"

Yeah, time to change the disposable contacts, my butt. I'll ask Dad later if he knows what's eating Mom. I swear, if this is all a plot to make me feel guilty and get me to stay home for college, I'll . . . I . . . I don't know what I'd do, honestly.

I sigh heavily so she'll know I'm not buying into her little act. Outside, we get into her car, and she notices something on the Chevy I'd hoped she wouldn't.

"*¿Y ese arañazo?*"

"What scratch?" I lean over her to see the thin wavy lines on the front right bumper of my truck. Great. Distract her. "I don't know! How'd that get there? I'll show Dad when we get back. Hurry, it's gonna rain."

Sedano's supermarket is always a circus. Ringmaster . . . clowns . . . everything. First, there's a DJ for 95.7 F.M., *El Sol* out front, drawing people to an already overpacked store with his superspeedy *merengue* music. Then, as the automatic doors slide open, the old *cubanazos* sip *café cubano* at a counter to my right, served by a woman with hair orange enough to make Lucille Ball roll in her grave. To my left, there's a line of men, practically drooling at my mom and me. No particular reason . . . we're female. And my absolute favorite—the ladies wearing workout shorts, *chancletas*, and giant rollers in their hair. What, if not for going out in public, are they doing their hair for? I mean, really. Did I mention all these people will buy lotto tickets before they leave the store?

Anyway, Mami decides to make *paella*. That way, if Andrew drops off some fish, she can use it in the dish. If not, it's still got the chicken, chorizo, and shrimp. In the middle of the produce section, there's a bin with both American and Cuban flags.

"Why do people here fly the Cuban flag?" I ask, tugging the fabric on one. Woops. I should've known better. Oh well, I already opened up the can of worms, guess I have to let them out now. "Isn't Cuba communist? So doesn't that make them communist, too?"

"*Mi vida*, it's not that simple. The Cuban flag means many things to many people, but mostly, it represents the people."

"But the people in Cuba are communist." Duh. And these plantains are way too ripe.

Mami bags them anyway for the *maduros*. "*Sí, pero* the people who display the flag here don't see communism, Isa. They see a place they once loved and still love."

"Yeah, but that place is now communist." I mean, helloooo?

She sighs, checking the firmness of a few tomatoes. "Isa, you don't understand. It's about honoring a memory of old Cuba. It's a need, *hija* . . . the power of need."

"You're right, Mami," I say, as I bag some fresh parsley. "I don't understand how people here can fly the Cuban flag, not the American flag, when America is the country that took them in. They wouldn't have anything without America, and yet, they wave the Cuban flag, a communist flag."

My mother sighs her oh-young-one-you-have-much-to-learn sigh. "*Primero*, the Cuban communist flag is red and black, okay?"

I love how she says okay. "Okay," I reply in her accent.

"Second, the Cubans here *do* fly the American flag. Just look at every other house on the street. But as for the Cuban flag . . ." She pauses to walk over and rip a couple more plastic baggies. "Let me ask you, Isa . . ."

See what I started? Me and my big, fat mouth.

She proceeds to choose the ripest green peppers from the bunch. "If, God forbid, something happened in this country, where there was a takeover of the government—"

"That would never happen," I interrupt.

"*Ah, sí?* How confident you are of that. I hope to God you're right, *mi hija*."

Jeez, would you look at these lovely hurricane candles with the Virgin Mary and all the saints on them? Supermarkets all across America should carry them.

"Just imagine it. Government takeover . . . and you had to move to another country to keep your *derechos humanos*, your human rights—"

"I know what *derechos humanos* are."

She stares at me.

Woops. "Sorry."

"You don't really want to know about this, Isa, *así que olvídate*. Forget it."

"No, sorry, Mom," I say again, remembering my dad and sister's warnings to go easy on my mom. "Please continue."

Her expression softens. "How would you feel seeing the American flag, *your* flag, after something like that happening? Would your feelings for it change? Or would you still love it? After all, it was not communist Americans who designed it, just as communist Cubans did not design *la de Cuba*."

Easy. "It would probably still make me proud, but I wouldn't wave it around, knowing it now represents something different."

She glances away, disappointed. We reach the deli counter, and she takes a number from the dispenser. She looks back at me, square in the eye. "I don't believe you, *hija*. You would wave it. And every time you saw it, you would think of America as you knew it, with its cities, and its *bitches* . . ."

"Beaches."

"And the movie theaters, and *el barrio* where you grew up, and your friends, *y tu familia*, and the hamburgers you love, and the *Kee line* pie, and how you could say anything and nobody would put you in jail for it. No matter where you end up living, this will always be your home, even if another nation was so kind as to take you in." She crosses her arms and turns to watch the numbers on the digital display.

I don't know. She's kind of right, but I still wouldn't fly the Cuban flag. It's communist! Then again, I've never known

Cuba any other way. But Mami has childhood memories there. Summers at the beach and all that. Maybe I do understand it a little, but still. "Whatever, Mami. I wasn't looking to argue with you."

"But we're not arguing! This is good. You need to see what we see."

"Who's *we*?"

"*Mi vida, los cubanos en el exilio.*"

"Mami, I'm not Cuban! I've never even seen Cuba with my own eyes!"

She faces me again and practically yells, but no one notices. Everyone here is practically yelling. It's the normal voice volume. "Isa! Yes, you are! *¡Tus padres son cubanos, tus abuelos son cubanos. Naciste aquí, pero nos tienes en tu sangre!* Open your eyes, *hija*! What are you so ashamed of?"

Next to me a lady is staring, waiting for my response. Her little girl clings to her leg as she sucks at a lollipop that stains her lips red.

I focus back on Mami's eyes. Rich, brown eyes, like looking into a mirror in the future. "Mami, I'm not ashamed of anything, okay? I love my family. I know we're not completely American, whatever that even means. I just wish sometimes you could be . . . a little less enthusiastic about Cuba. It makes me wonder if you wouldn't move there again once things are back to normal."

She laughs softly, but it's not real. "Things will never go back to normal, Isa. And if they do, I won't be around to see it."

The other lady smiles at me, at least it looks like a faint smile, and reaches up to the counter to receive her package. She walks off with her daughter skipping behind.

"*Sí, yo sé que* I'm enthusiastic, *pero* maybe if you loved your heritage as much as we do, I wouldn't have to try so hard."

Oh. So that's why she does it? Because she thinks I'm not enthusiastic enough? Because she thinks I don't care? Well, hey, if that's all. Fine, a little enthusiasm, maestro.

I reach into yet another bin of Cuban flags, pull one out, and wave it high in circles and plaster a grin on my face. "*¡Viva Cuba libre!*" I announce to everyone within hearing range, and a few butchers from the meat department cheer.

Mami shields her eyes and shakes her head. "*Loca.*"

Eleven

Where's my fine brush? Oh, there it is. I'm dying to finish this painting already, so I can start a new one when I get to Michigan. The scenery will be different, so it wouldn't make any sense to finish this sandy landscape up there. The whole vibe will be different, like between my mom and me and the whole Sedano's discussion yesterday. You'd think, as the baby in the family, that I'd get along better with her, but we've always lived in different worlds.

Like I remember when I was little . . . I used to *love* lighting a candle on stormy nights and walking around the house in my long nightgown, pretending to be an actress in some old movie, a visitor at a mad scientist's castle. Every now and then, I'd stop and strike a pose for the imaginary camera before wandering on. My final destination was always the bookcase in our den, the scientist's secret library. Then I'd hear eerie violin music coming from somewhere within the walls. And just as I'd be about to pull the book on human anatomy (which was really a switch to a secret passageway), Mami would suddenly fling open the door, flick on the light, and demand, "*¿Isabelita, que estás haciendo?*"

"Nothing," I'd say, and just like that, I was jolted back into reality, into her world.

It's sort of the same thing with my family. Am I Cuban or American? Where do I belong? I was born here, but if I say I'm American, it'll draw *no, mi vida* looks from my folks. If I say I'm Cuban, that wouldn't make any sense either, since the closest I've come to seeing the island was with binoculars on a cruise ship one summer. But I have to know and be comfortable with it before I go to Michigan. Because here, I feel the most *gringa* of all my family, but there, I'll be the Latina girl with an accent I never knew I had.

Why do I think about such lame things when I'm painting? I have to stop staring at this canvas and start already. Maybe I should add something unique to this storm scene, but what?

"Hey, Isa." Andrew's here—pulling off his orange poncho in the middle of the art room. Talk about being in my own world. I didn't even hear him come in.

"Hey, sweetie!" Whoa, I just called him sweetie.

He looks tired. I totally understand; it's been a long day. He also looks major hot with that new haircut.

"I've been dying to see you," he says, inching over to my easel, taking the brush right out of my hand, and tossing it aside.

God, help me. "Really?"

"Yes, really." He drops his face to mine and pulls me close. And that's the extent of the conversation.

We probably shouldn't be doing this here, with staff members nearby. But that thought goes away quickly, replaced with feelings I never knew I had. Every inch of my body is alive. I always thought that phrase sounded corny in love songs, but I get it now. The butterflies are back, frantically flapping their little wings inside me, as if trying to warn me. About what, I have no idea. Because if there *is* something wrong with Andrew, I just don't care anymore.

Twelve

Dad loves Home Depot, especially on Monday nights. It's the hardest day of the week for him, so he likes to unwind by taking in the scent of freshly sawed plywood. Me, I like the paint aisles. Maybe I'll start getting ideas for the mural I plan to do in my future home.

Whenever I have a problem or something I don't want to tell my mom about, I talk to Dad at Home Depot. I wonder if he has any wisdom regarding Coach.

"Dad, you know Andrew?"

"Andrew? *Sí, cómo no, ¿qué le pasa?*"

"Nothing's wrong with him." Dad always has to ask what's wrong with everybody. The family fixer-upper. "That's the problem—nothing's wrong with him."

"*¿Qué quiere decir eso?*"

"Well, I mean, I really like him. He's great, he's funny,

he's smart, helpful . . ."

I won't mention how he makes me . . . Okay, no. I definitely can't tell my father how I have to change my panties after almost every time I'm with Andrew.

"And I shouldn't like him. He lives here, goes to school here, and soon I'll be gone. See what I mean?"

"So what do you want to do, *hija*?" he asks as we turn into the bath appliance aisle.

"I don't know, I don't know." I run my finger along the dusty shelving, leaving a long, clean trail. "What should I do? Should I not be seeing him?"

"For now? I don't see why not. You'll just have to decide what to do when your time's up, that's all."

Huh? Is he even listening? He checks out the faucets on sale. For whose bathroom, I don't know. All our faucets are pretty new, but I forget that my dad's on this endless quest to accumulate spare parts in our garage. "*Pero* listen," he says, eyebrows drawing close.

Uh-oh. I hope what's coming next doesn't involve the word *contraceptivo*.

"I need to sit with you and Stefan soon to discuss something."

Discuss something? How has my boyfriend dilemma made him think of something he needs to discuss with me and Stefan? Could he be any less interested in my problem? "Like what, Papi?"

"Eh, it's better if we talk about it with Stefan." He turns the faucet box around to read the back.

He's gotta be kidding. "What's so important that we have to have a meeting with Stefan? Why can't you just tell me now?"

I hate when he does this. He brings up something that sounds important, then doesn't tell me what it is. How cruel is that?

"*Nada, chica*. I'm sorry I said anything. We'll talk about it soon."

"Dad? Don't do that. That's so mean." But he doesn't reply. It'll have to wait.

We pay for the new faucet and show our receipt at the exit. I hate these people. What is their main purpose anyway? They don't really look at your receipt, and they don't check your bag, either. They just punch a hole in the stupid paper with their stupid pen.

What the heck could my dad have to say?

It's 8:30, and the sun is going down. The sky's mottled with pink and purple clouds, framed by pine trees along the canal. We're chugging back home in the Chevy. Dad hasn't mentioned anything since we left the store, and I know better than to bring it up again. He'll speak when he so chooses, not when I give him the evil eye.

This must be my lucky night, because his mouth opens.

"*Mira*, Isa . . . you're right. I should talk to you now, not with Stefan. But I don't want you to panic, *porque* that would only make your mother worse."

Panic?

"Eh . . ." He rubs his brow.

Dad's never had trouble spitting something right out. Why's he even setting this up? Of course, my fingers head straight for my earlobe.

"*Hija*, some time ago, Mami had her annual . . . you know, *mamografía*." He pauses. In my peripheral vision, I can see him turning his face to me, maybe for any sign of understanding to make this easier on him.

But I say nothing. I stare straight ahead. A few feet in front of us a cat scrambles across the street, and I don't even flinch.

"The results showed . . ."

He just better not say it.

"A mass."

I turn to look at him. I can feel my bottom lip trembling. "What?"

The silence in the car is unsettling. Dad continues to drive, looking forward with stony eyes. God, please tell me this is all a joke. No, it can't be. Dad would never . . .

"No." I stare at him blankly, the contour of his nose, the stubble on his face. *A mass*. This can't be happening. Not my mom. I lower my face into my hands and start crying right there, without thinking anymore, without asking for details.

I stare back at him through tears, the streetlights sparkling like starbursts. He's watching the road again, one hand on the wheel, one waving around, trying to express what his words can't. "It was small, Isa. They took a sample with a thin needle. In and out procedure."

"You mean a biopsy? Mami had a biopsy, and I didn't know?"

Silence.

"Why hasn't she told me this, Dad? When did this happen? Does Carmen know?"

"Yes. *Hija*, she didn't tell you because she didn't want you to worry. It might not have been anything, but—"

It might not have been anything. "But it is," I interrupt, searching his face. "That's what you're going to say, isn't it? It's cancer."

He says nothing.

"Why?" I shout. The sobs come full force this time, so hard I can barely breathe. "She doesn't deserve it!"

All of a sudden images of Mami flicker through my mind—of her singing *Sapo Verde* at my ninth birthday party with a handkerchief in her hair, looking like a movie star, clapping and laughing. Another of her lying next to me in my little bed, just barely fitting, holding me close when I had the flu. She didn't care if she got sick, she just wanted to comfort me because of how bad I felt. At the fair, when I caught her dabbing her eyes looking at my painting of that stupid bird.

I don't believe this! I can't lose my mom! I just can't!

"*Mi hija*," my dad says, putting his hand at the nape of my neck and kneading my skin, "Mami's not going to die, okay?"

Oh, great. That makes me cry even more. The words "Mami" and "die" in the same sentence are unbearable. I can't speak. Nothing comes out, only sobs and more sobs.

He goes on. "They're going to remove the lump and some tissue around it. After that, they'll treat her to make sure it doesn't spread into the . . . *¿cómo se llama eso?*"

"Lymph nodes." It comes out a whisper. It was in the brochure I read when I went in for my first Pap smear. I remember reading all about breast cancer, never thinking for one second that the info would come to haunt me later. Or my mom, rather. It was the only thing left to read in that little waiting room.

"Right. They found it early. *Dijeron que era* Stage 1."

My heart eases up a little. I read that women in this stage have a really good chance of surviving. "When? When are they removing it?"

"Her surgery is the twenty-ninth. A Thursday."

"Are they going to remove her breast?"

I *cannot* believe I'm asking this question. This is just not happening.

"No, it's partial—lumpectomy. After that they'll start her on radiation."

I just don't believe this. "But Dr. Hernández the other day—"

"She didn't see Dr. Hernández, Isa. She went to an oncologist, a Dr. Weiss."

An oncologist? All this has been going on, and I haven't known anything? This is why my dad and Carmen have been asking me to take it easy?

"*Hija, no te preocupes.* She's going to be okay. I know it. Your mother has a strong will."

No kidding, and it's always been her will against mine, which I've always hated. But now, when she'll need it most, it better come into play. She just better kick this in the ass, or . . . or I don't know what I'll do.

The rest of the ride is silent, except for my sniffling. The sun is completely gone now, though some deep purple sky still remains. My father must figure he's given me enough to think about, as he goes through routine motions—putting on the indicator, turning onto our street, stopping at a stop sign.

But inside me, nothing's routine anymore. Suddenly, the stupid things I've always wanted seem so small. How am I supposed to leave now with her like this? What good is all that independence if I lose my mom? There'd be no one to be independent from. What now? I never expected this.

This totally changes everything.

Thirteen

Later that night I walk into Stefan's room and find him in his boxers, sitting on the edge of his bed with his head in his hands. He senses me and looks up. His eyes are all red, his face all wet.

"You're not going out?" I ask.

Stefan shakes his head, then drops it again. His whole body shudders.

I go over, sit next to him, and run my fingers through his hair. He has really nice hair, my brother does. "She's going to make it, nerdhead," I tell him, fighting the nagging feeling in my stomach that it might not be true.

Stefan leans into me and sobs even more.

This is gonna hurt.

"Mami?"

"Mmm?" she answers with eyes closed, head back on her pillow.

I settle next to her on the bed. "I'm calling U-M tomorrow and letting them know I won't be there for the fall semester." The words are painful, but I can't leave now. It wouldn't feel right, not to mention the guilt trip would be from here to Mongolia.

On TV David Letterman is delivering a monologue, but Mami has the show on mute, so all you see is Letterman pausing for the audience's reaction and straightening his suit. Paul Shaffer says something, and his drummer hits a cymbal.

"*Isa, no seas boba,*" Mami says, running her fingers through my hair. "I'll be fine."

I nestle deeper into her arms. "I'm not leaving you like this."

"This shouldn't change anything." She sighs.

"Shouldn't change anything?" I look up into her warm brown eyes—eyes that'll always be with me anywhere I go. "Are you crazy? Of course it does, Mami."

"*Mi vida*, do whatever you were going to do before this happened, okay? If you want to go, go. If you want to stay, of course I'm not going to stop you. *¿Tú me entiendes?*"

You see? That's all she had to say. I know she wants me here with her. "I understand what you're saying, but my mind's already made up. I'm not going to Michigan now. I'm staying to take care of you." Letterman is now acting like Elvis, rotating his hips and doing karate chops in the air.

"*Isa, yo sé que tú me quieres, hija, pero* please don't stay

103

because of me. I know you have your own life, *mi vida.*"

She's testing me. I know it. She really wants me to stay and *not* have Carmen's attitude. She wants me to be by her side, not abandon her. It's a guilt thing.

"Don't worry, Mami. I can always enroll later. This comes first." I can't believe there's no U-M now. God, this all sucks so bad.

She says nothing.

Somewhere during Letterman's Top Ten, Mami starts humming an old Cuban folk song, one I've heard a million times but could never tell you the name. Doesn't matter, anyway, it always lulls me to sleep. And that's where I end up spending the night—in my mother's arms, between her and Dad, just like being six again.

When I wake up in the morning, I'm still in my parents' bed, but Mami's gone. I run to her closet. It's empty. A hanger swings softly, as if someone has just pulled off the last item in the closet and left. I sprint to the kitchen, but the lights are off, and so are the Cuban coffeemaker and the range. No smells waft throughout the house. No piles of folded laundry on the sofa. Nothing . . . except a hollow echo when I cry for her.

When I wake up for real, I'm alone in their bed. I can hear my dad in the shower and Mami's clanking in the kitchen. My heart lifts as my eyes spill over. She's still here. Thank you, Lord.

• • • ● • • •

At camp this morning I passed Susy in the hallway, and she went, "Hello," in the most annoying way, like I've hurt her or don't trust her judgment or something. You know, I don't need that kind of attitude right now, with everything going on. So Andrew wants to be with me and not her. So what?

The rest of the day I've thought of nothing but the feeling of emptiness I had in last night's dream. How our home wouldn't be the same without Mami. It made me feel stronger about staying in Miami, even though I know what I'll be giving up. Once I know she'll be okay, I'll enroll. Maybe in the winter.

My painting's really coming alive now. The sense of longing I wanted is starting to show. Surrounding the girl is the most beautiful beach with fine sands and majestic palm trees, but overhead the sky is dark. The seas are choppy. I'm adding the white froth on the waves, trying to get them to look like they're churning just right, when Andrew knocks on the open door.

"Hey!" He drags in his equipment bag and just stands there. "What happened last night? I called you but your mom said you weren't home. So I called again later and your brother told me you'd call me back. So I got worried and e-mailed you, but you didn't—"

"I'm sorry, Andrew." I wipe the paintbrush on a paper towel. "Something came up." I chew my lower lip and fight back the urge to lose it. Too late. My eyes are brimming.

He drops his bag and rushes over. "Isa, what happened? Are you okay?" He takes the brush out of my hands and gently holds my face.

I shake my head. "My mom has breast cancer. I just found out." I wipe tears away and fling them aside. "Apparently she's known this for a few weeks but didn't tell me. She's going in for surgery on the twenty-ninth to remove a lump."

Andrew tilts his head. He looks straight into my face, almost like he's trying to see through it. He points a finger at me, just like on our first date. "You're not . . ."

"Of course I'm not kidding."

"Just checking." He lets go of a deep breath and pulls me close, softly pushing my head to rest on his shoulder. "I'm so sorry, baby."

Baby. And that's how I feel, too, like a big baby. I cry into his shoulder, breathing in the earthy smell of his neck. Because he's been outside all day, the very scent of the swamp has imprinted itself into his skin.

"Is there anything I can do?"

I think about this, but of course there isn't. "No," I say, giving in to his arms, letting go of the tension that's suffocating me. "Just stay with me."

God, I can't remember the last time I cried this much in two days. I didn't even cry when I broke up with Robi. I felt bad for having hurt him, but the tears didn't come.

After a few minutes I wipe my face and force a weak smile. "Sorry. I soaked your shirt."

He looks at his shoulder and laughs. "You don't have to be sorry. Look, Isa," he says, taking my hands and leaning back on a table. "This is your mom you're talking about. If you need space, I understand. I can back off."

It's funny . . . in a way, I kind of do need my space. I should be making my life as uncomplicated as possible right now in order to help Mom. But another part of me—a big part of me—needs Andrew. I need his jokes, his shoulder, his beautiful eyes, his hands. Besides, I can indulge in him now. I'm not leaving anymore.

"Coach, listen, I've sort of decided, okay, I've definitely decided, not to go to Michigan for the fall semester. With all this going on, I just need to hang around for a while, until I feel sure that she'll be all right."

He stares at me like he's just heard the dumbest thing ever. "You're kidding."

"No, why?"

"Why would you do that? You're registered and everything's planned out. You're set to go."

"Because I can't go with her like this. I can't, Andrew."

"Yeah, but I've always admired that about you. The way you think so differently from your mom, no offense . . . the way you're willing to stand up for your beliefs and are so sure of what you want. Now you're just going to forget all that?"

"Of course not, but what am I supposed to do? Just leave her? She needs me. Believe me, it kills me that I'm not going now, but I can't. I just can't."

"I understand you feel obligated to stay, but wouldn't she want you to go anyway? I mean, it's your college education."

I laugh. "Uh, no. You don't know my mom." But then I remember last night when she told me that I should go anyway. Was that for real? Probably not. That was just reverse psychology at its finest. I think.

"Seriously. Wouldn't she want you to go on with your life and not worry about her? I know my mom would."

"Andrew, you don't understand. Going away to college isn't such a big thing in our family. Education is, but going away to get it isn't. In fact, most people I graduated with are going to Florida International University and Miami-Dade just to stay close to their families. Family is a big deal to us, in case you haven't noticed."

"Oh, and what are you saying? That family isn't important to a *gringo* like me?"

"No, that's not what I'm saying. *¡Ay!*" I stamp my foot on the concrete floor. "It's just different between you and me sometimes, okay? Like, when was the last time you talked to your mom? Or your dad?"

"What does that have to do with anything?"

"Just answer. Think, when was the last time?"

"I don't know, two weeks ago, but so what? That doesn't mean I love my folks any less than you do yours."

"Of course not, that's not what I'm saying. But look, if I moved to Michigan, even with that great feeling of independence and all, I'd still be calling my mom every other night just to hear her voice. That's how it is with us. My cousin Lloyd goes to FSU in Tallahassee, but he drives home for every long weekend, holiday, and sometimes just for the hell of it. He just can't stay away."

He stops to ponder this. "You have a cousin named Lloyd?"

Silence.

"Shut up, dork." I punch his arm.

"Ow!" He doubles up laughing. "All right, Isa, I don't want to argue with you. All I'm saying is maybe you should give it some time. Let a few days pass. You're in shock, but that shouldn't make you change your plans for college. That's just how I feel."

"Look, you want me to go? Is that it? 'Cause I thought you'd be happy that I'm staying. Besides, I didn't say it was forever, just until she's better."

"Of course I don't want you to go. It's just that . . . well, I think it's what's best for you. But hey, what do I know?" He smiles and takes my hands again. "You're a smart girl. And a smart girl will make a smart decision. Do what you feel is right, babe."

I wasn't really asking for his advice on the matter, but still, it's nice to know he cares about me. "That's better. You were starting to scare me there." I walk closer to him and press my body against his, lowering my head to kiss him for the first time since Friday.

"So I guess you're going to spend the weekend with your mom and forget me, huh?"

Go away. Forget me. Good God, Andrew, shut up already.

"Actually my mom insisted I go out this weekend; that I can't help by keeping surveillance over her. So why don't we do something Friday?"

"Uh . . . okay. Movie?" he asks.

I caress his arms softly. I remember seeing these solid

arms the first day of camp, and now they're here in front of me, and I'm caressing them. So weird sometimes to think that we're actually together. Me and Mystery Man, Underwear Ad Guy. "Sure, but why don't we rent one and take it to your place? You've never invited me over."

He stares. Underneath his brow, his eyes are sullen but sexy. "I didn't want you getting the wrong impression."

Where've I heard that before? "Now you sound like my mother." Behind him I catch a glimpse of the clock, high on the wall. 5:45. "Damn, I didn't realize it was so late. I didn't even finish this."

I think Andrew stopped listening to me after I said "your place." Without another word he pulls me to him, and I can feel that I was right. His kiss is more intense than ever. There's something behind it, raw and simple, something out of a human sexuality textbook. He doesn't need to say anything. I feel it too. I don't know how far we'll go on Friday, but this much I know—

I want him. Bad.

Fourteen

Andrew's apartment is right near UM. It's also dangerously close to the Big Cheese, the best pizza place in the history of pizza places. Andrew and I eat there, splitting a ham and pineapple, which is cool because Robi never liked anything but plain cheese. After talking about my mom for a while, we head to the video store and rent a DVD, although we probably won't be watching it anyway.

He pushes his key in and unlocks the door to his apartment. Slowly he swings it open. When the lights come on, I get my first look at his place. Nice and neat. The carpet has vacuum cleaner marks. There's a sofa, a love seat, and a dinette next to the kitchen, complete with fresh flowers just for me. Of course, there's also a basketball hoop on the wall in the living room.

"Welcome to my underground lair," he says in a Dr. Evil-like voice.

Let's just hope his bedroom doesn't look anything like Austin Powers's. If I see one psychedelic anything, I'm outta here. "Very nice, Coach," I say, stepping in. "I like the hoop."

He throws the DVD onto the sofa. "Gotta have a hoop, right?" He gestures to the room with open arms, then lets them fall to his sides. "This is it. Make yourself at home. I'll be right back." He walks across the living room and opens the door to his bedroom.

I feel weird just standing here, so I stroll around. On the walls he's got some framed posters of the Dolphins and Panthers. No photos of family, as far as I can see. There's a chenille throw on the sofa, which looks extremely comfy, not to mention girly. That and the flowers. Otherwise, anyone wondering if the apartment belonged to a guy or girl need only look at the basketball hoop. Or the five remote controls on the coffee table.

Five remote controls. I laugh to myself. I wonder which one brings the lights down and the slow jams up. I sit on the edge of the sofa.

Andrew comes back, closing the bedroom door. "Sorry. I was checking messages. Want something to drink?"

"Nah, thanks." My hands are slippery. I blot them against my shorts.

"If you get thirsty, I've got whatever. Coke, Sprite, Bacardi, vodka . . . a full minibar," he says with a laugh.

I fight the urge to pull my earlobe. I don't want him thinking I'm nervous, because I'm not. Not really. I'm not nervous. Okay, a little. "Thanks, I'll let you know."

"Ready to watch the movie?" He picks up the case and squats in front of the TV. While waiting for the player to turn on, he glances my way. "All the booze I've got is beer, Isa. I was only kidding about the minibar." He pushes a button, and the disc tray ejects.

"I know!" No, I don't. But how does he know that, that I took him seriously? It must be all over my face. *Relax, Isa.*

The disc tray slides back in. "Don't worry, I'm not going to corrupt Mami's little girl and send her home drunk. I wouldn't do anything to jeopardize being with you, *señorita.*"

"I know." I'm extremely witty tonight with all these *I knows.* Still, corrupting me a little won't hurt anyone.

He comes and sits next to me, picking up one of the remotes and pushing all kinds of buttons. If I had to repeat what he's doing to save the world from a comet collision, we'd all be dead. Why don't they make remote controls with only one button? Turn on, turn off. Okay, and volume buttons, too.

The movie comes on, warning us about the FBI and copyrights. His arm reaches around me to grab the throw on my other side.

"'Scuse me," he says, pulling the end of it from under my butt. He smiles and kisses my cheek.

Sigh.

I sink into the sofa. Immediately my muscles relax. I have to admit, the thought of Andrew being twenty-three makes me nervous sometimes, like I'm doing something wrong. I know Mami wouldn't like it, which is exactly why I'm not telling her, but otherwise, she seems to tolerate him just fine.

113

Even though it's only been less than a month since we've been going out, I can't imagine *not* being with him right now.

I'll see how far we get tonight. Not as far as he might hope, no matter how randy I feel. That, I'll save for a couple weeks from now, if I can take it. Tonight I just wanna see what's under those clothes, even if it means there'll be no tab-A-into-slot-B.

"Andrew."

"Yes, ma'am?"

"You know, with all our talking, I've never asked you something."

"I'm twenty-three."

"No, dummy." I laugh, pinching his side—his hard side, the one with not an ounce of fat on it. "I've never asked you about girlfriends."

"Girlfriends?" He readjusts himself.

"Well, yeah. I'm assuming you've had a relationship before."

He lifts a finger, and in a college professor voice, says, "Ah, but to assume means to make an 'ass' out of 'u' and 'me.' "

Oh, jeez. I need no funniness for just a minute. "Coach? I'm serious."

He lets out a sigh. "Sorry. Why do you assume?"

"Because! What girl wouldn't want to be with you?"

"Well, maybe I haven't wanted a relationship."

Something in his eyes . . . Yes, he's joking, the stupid nerd. "Yeah, right."

He smiles, but then his gaze drops to his lap, and he

straightens the bottom of his shirt. "I'm just kidding. Yes, I had a girlfriend once. We were together for three years, but she left me. She was a bitch anyway." He laughs again. It's not a real laugh, though. His eyes glint of hurt.

"You don't mean that, right?"

"Nah, she was a nice girl. I guess I wasn't right for her."

Which suddenly makes me feel guilty. Why? Because I've done the same? Is Robi sitting somewhere tonight, telling some girl how much he hates me because I thought we should move on?

"Oh. Well, I'm sorry about that," I say, almost as if I was the one responsible for their breakup. "Was she the only one?"

"Pretty much. She was my first. I was nineteen when she left."

Which means he's been solo for four years. "So . . ."

"I've seen other people since then."

People. He says *people* instead of *girls*, like that would hurt me. "Girls."

"Yes, girls. Women."

Hold up. "Women?"

"Isa . . ." He tilts his face and takes a good look at me. "What are you getting at?"

"I'm sorry, am I being nosy? We talk about everything else; I didn't think you'd mind. I just wanted to know."

"Well, there's not much to tell. I just haven't found the right girl yet."

In the meantime, though, he's been having the time of his

life. He must have. He can't look the way he does and not get it on a regular basis. I must find out. "You can talk to me, Andrew. You know that. Don't think I'll be hurt by anything you have to say. I know you've probably had sex a million times—it's all right."

He throws his head back and laughs. "I haven't had sex a million times. I'm only in the hundred-thousands."

I laugh. On the outside. Yeah, that's hilarious. But inside, scenes of Andrew with different girls invade my mind. For some reason, I don't see their faces, just girls, on their backs, on top of him, and Andrew pleasing them till they scream. On one hand, the thoughts make me cringe, while on the other . . . *Whoa, Isa, slow down.*

At least with Robi, I knew what I was getting. He'd been with one girl before me, and that was it. But Andrew . . . who knows. The hundred-thousand estimate is probably not that far off. Maybe I really don't want to know how many girls he's been with.

There's an awkward hush. Andrew knows what's on my mind. He tries changing the focus. "What about you, missy? Who've you been with, besides Pool Boy?"

"Pool Boy." I remember Robi stepping back, his napkin and plate flying everywhere, and the splash. I can't believe some people actually thought I did that. That was all him and his klutzy ass. "Before him, I only went on a few dates, but that was it. I was young."

I was young, I say, as if I'm ninety years old, remembering the glory days.

At this, Andrew coughs a laugh. "You were young! God, that's too cute."

Great, now he thinks I'm a sweet little girl with stupid things to say. I pull my earlobe.

He must feel bad for laughing, because he grabs my hand and gets serious again. "So you've only been with him?"

"Yes."

"And was that good or bad?"

Good or bad. "What do you mean?"

"Was he good to you? You know." His eyebrows go up, and I can tell he's really asking if Robi did more for me than just write love notes.

I pause for a moment, remembering the times Robi and I had messed around. He tried. He really did. "He was okay," I say.

He nods for a moment, interpreting the answer quietly. "That's a no."

I look down at our hands. Our skin is so different. His is tanned and drier, from being out there all day on the field. Mine's lighter, from painting indoors and not getting out enough.

"I guess." It's all I can say. I mean, he's right. I always had to take care of myself after Robi went home, while he left feeling fine and dandy.

"Let me know," he says, sweeping a strand of hair and tucking it behind my ear. He looks at my lips.

"Let you know what?" I ask stupidly.

His forehead touches mine, his eyes watch me intently.

"Let me know when you're ready for more than okay."

A rush of ripples heads straight for the center of my body. They come faster this time. I hold Andrew's face in my gaze for a moment and check it to make sure he's not kidding. And because I see nothing more than want, and need, and eyes that've done nothing but mesmerize me for weeks, I give in.

I grab him and pull him toward me, kissing and teasing. Andrew yields easily, and I realize this is what they mean by *putty in your hands*. He's doing nothing but kissing back, happily accepting my hands as they move over his chest, onto his stomach, and under his shirt to feel his warmth.

Almost like he's not sure, his hand wanders over my shoulder, waiting for some kind of clue, worried of any further feel. Worried about my age. It's the only reason he's not searching for more, because his body is telling me otherwise. I can feel it when I lean into him, but still, he's holding back.

I stop long enough to whisper, "I'll be eighteen in three weeks."

Breathing quickly, he nods. And that does the trick. Andrew's out of the hold, gripping my face, moving his mouth harder over mine, tasting and kissing. I push into him, and he slides his hands along my neck, shoulders, stopping to cup my breast softly. My hand moves over his, urging him to squeeze harder. Then he reaches around and caresses my back and butt. There he grips me tight, releasing his kiss and biting his own lip with a sly smile.

Let me know when you're ready for more than okay. His words are ringing in my ears. I'm more than ready. I'm way overdue.

As Andrew softly bites my neck, I glance up long enough to see some guy chasing some other guy on the TV, followed by a loud crash and a huge explosion. And then Andrew's phone starts ringing. Stupid phone. But he's a good boy for not answering it. The machine in his room picks up, and I can just barely hear a girl's voice leaving a message.

"Aaghh," he says into my hair. "My little sis."

I smile and quickly push the image of his sister out of my head, hands going back to exploring his body, as my mouth searches his again. I can't help but feel a bit of satisfaction knowing that Susy would love to be in my place right now—running my hand along his thigh, up to the top of his shorts, pausing to feel the sensitive skin underneath his zipper.

Fifteen

People without pools always talk about how cool it would be to have a pool. People with pools hardly ever use them. Today I feel like using ours. Not a cloud in the sky, Mami says she's feeling pretty good, and so am I. When I left Andrew's last night, I had to think of anything but his bare body to keep from running red lights. Third base is a pretty cool place to be with Andrew Corbin.

"Isa!"

Is someone calling me? I'm not sure with this radio blaring.

"Isaaaa!" Mami hollers from inside the house.

"*¡Aquí, Mami!*" I yell back. The water's great. I think I'll stay here till I prune up.

"*Allí está.*" I hear her telling someone where I'm hiding. She stands at the sliding glass door, waiting for someone to catch up with her.

Who's she talking to? Through the glare, I see Robi step onto the patio. He walks up to the edge of the pool, hands in his shorts pockets.

"Hey, what're you doing here?" I ask. I mean, really. What the hell?

"Hi, Isa. How are you?"

"Fine." Though I'm not sure why we're even having this conversation. "Robi, it would be nice if you called first."

"Why?" he asks with a fake smile. "So you can hide your boyfriend?"

I check my bikini to make sure everything's in place. It's so weird to see him. Like he's a stranger. It's also weird that he's seeing me half naked, even though he's seen me half naked before. "So what's up?"

"I heard about your mom. I'm sorry."

"Oh. I think she'll be fine. She's strong." Is that why he came by? I stand there, shielding the sun from my eyes. "If you're going to stay, can you please sit over there so I don't have to squint?"

Without answering, he takes a seat underneath the patio table umbrella. My eyes follow, praying he won't fall in the pool again. I wade toward him, splash the brick border with water, so I don't burn my elbows. He wants to talk again. The last time was the week after the prom, when I asked that we not talk for a while. I guess he figures *a while* is over.

He's quiet at first. Then, "Isa, what are you doing?"

I blink. "Excuse me?"

He looks at me all serious. "Just tell me straight out. Are

you going out with that guy?"

"You mean Andrew?" Yikes, that name alone probably kills him. Maybe I shouldn't have said it. "Yes."

He looks away. Why is he torturing himself like this? I'm not going to lie to him. Whatever he asks me, I'm going to tell the truth.

"Why, Isa?" He leans forward, hands clasped in front of him. "You said you needed to breathe. You said it wasn't me, it was space you wanted, and now you're going out with that dude? I don't understand."

"Robi . . ." How do I say this? "That's what I thought. But then I met him at work, and I like him, okay? I know that must sound really bad to you, but I'm sorry. It just happened."

"You're sorry." He laughs. "Yeah, okay, you look real sorry."

"What's that supposed to mean?"

"How sorry could you possibly be, Isa?"

I don't know where he's going with this. His tone is freaking me out.

"I saw you," he says.

"Saw me? Where?"

He bites his lip, leaning back in the chair, trying real hard not to cry. He also looks to see if anyone else is around. "At the freakin' guy's apartment."

No, he didn't. "You what?" I yell. "You followed me? What the hell's wrong with you? You could be arrested for that, Robi!"

He shoots out of his chair. "Dammit, Isa, I miss you!

I . . . screw it, I love you."

"Oh, Jesus."

"Oh, Jesus, what? Why the hell did you end it? There was nothing wrong with us."

"There was nothing right, either!" I can't believe he's doing this! Why can't he just let go already?

He looks down at his sneakers, letting it sink in. "So . . . how was he?"

I don't like his voice. I've never heard Robi like this. He's hurt and pissed, and I know what's coming next.

"Was he good? Did he do it for you? Did he make you—"

"Shut up! Get the hell out of here right now!" My hand flies out of the water, spraying drops everywhere.

"Answer me!"

"Get the hell out, Robi. I can't believe you did such a shitty thing and now you're asking me this," I hiss at him, tears brimming at my eyes. "It's not like you."

"Yeah?" he asks. "Well, maybe I haven't been myself lately. Do you have any idea what it's like to know that someone else is screwing my girlfriend?"

"Robi—"

"That someone who couldn't care less about you is using you and you don't even know it?"

"Stop it. You're just pissed."

"Pissed? No, no, Isa, I'm not pissed. I'm freakin' falling apart, okay? Every single day, every weekend, every time I check my phone, my e-mail, only to find that you still haven't called, that you don't care about me, even

123

though I treated you right."

"We're not screwing," I say, to use his choice of words. He's never said that to describe sex before.

"Well, you sure as hell aren't eating ice-cream cones at his place at one o'clock in the morning."

"Stop it! Don't follow me again. This isn't about you."

"Bullshit!"

"Shhh!"

He quiets down and paces the tile in front of me. "You know . . . if you just would have told me that you wanted someone else or that I wasn't making you happy, then fine, but you said you wanted to be free. You're not free. You're with someone else already, so it must have been me. You were just too chicken to say it."

Ouch.

He didn't have to throw that in my face. I know I told him that, and I know that I wanted to be free, but things didn't go as planned. Maybe I should've waited longer before finding someone new. Maybe I am the jerk here.

"I met someone else, Robi. I know it hurts to hear that."

"You don't know anything." He glares at me.

In a million years, I never thought I'd see Robi glaring at me.

"I won't follow you anymore, trust me. I'm over this." He turns around and walks off. The patio door slides open, and he pauses, looking at me with the most pain I've ever seen on his face.

He better not say he loves me, because it won't make this

any easier. I just don't feel the same anymore. But he doesn't say anything. He walks into the house, and he's gone.

For the rest of the day I replay the argument over and over in my head. His words . . . *Someone who couldn't care less about you is using you.* I know he only said it because he was mad. So then why does it bother me so much?

Sixteen

It's Stefan's twenty-second birthday. We're heading to the Melting Pot for dinner, then he's off to South Beach. He would invite me along, he says, except I won't be able to get into any clubs. I know Susy never found this to be a problem when she was seventeen. She'd find fake IDs from anyone.

The ride to the restaurant seems long. My hands are sweaty. This is the second time Andrew will be joining us for some family fun. Since the day after the barbecue, Mom hasn't asked again how old he is, and I know it's because she's been so distracted with her own worries. I'm just hoping she won't ask before my birthday, when I can say I'm eighteen and can date whoever I want.

At the restaurant they seat us at a superhuge booth, in part because we're a large group, but also because Stefan's date's butt is so big. Where he picked this one up, I have no idea. All

I know is she's very happy to be meeting the folks. My parents are all over her, asking questions in Spanish, laughing like she'd make the perfect *nuera*. They don't realize Stefan will never get married. And from the way she's got her arm hooked around his, giggling at his every stupid joke, neither does she.

Also joining us are my cousins Michael, Gabriel, and Lucas. All over twenty-one. All will be getting sloshed with Stefan tonight. These are my *tía* Clarita's kids, from my dad's side of the family. We don't know many people from my mom's side. Both of her parents died in Cuba. She came to Miami with *Tío* Raul when she was nineteen, and he died a few years ago. At least that's what I've always heard.

I'm telling Andrew all of this when the waitress comes up, introduces herself as Maria, and tells us the specials. Suddenly it occurs to me that I have about ten seconds to tell Andrew something before she starts taking drink orders.

I lean over and whisper, "Don't order a beer tonight."

For a moment he's in a trance. He whispers back, "Why?"

"Just don't. I haven't told my parents yet how old you are."

He looks at me. "Wouldn't they know anyway? I don't look seventeen, do I?"

I raise my eyebrows and lean into him. "Definitely not."

Under the table, he squeezes my thigh.

As the waitress jots down the orders, I notice her long, shiny, black hair, pulled into a sleek ponytail. Her eyebrows are perfectly shaped over bright green eyes, and her full lips have a deep color of their own. She's also got a nice body, and that's with only boring black pants, a white shirt, and an apron on. Normally I don't get jealous, but all the guys are noticing her, including Andrew.

Stefan's date, who I'll call Booty, since I still don't know her name, is looking around at all the faces, just like I am, so in a matter of seconds, she sees me looking at her. She raises her eyebrows, shaking her head, like *Can you believe these guys?*

I give her an empathetic look. "Ahem," I say to Andrew. It's his turn to order something.

"I'll just have water," he says with a smile.

Maria nods and smiles back. Maybe I should be proud that other girls check out my boyfriend. Maybe I should gloat that he's mine, all mine. But I'm not. I can't help but hate Maria the Waitress, even though she's done absolutely nothing wrong.

"*An-drroo?*" It's my mom, actually speaking to my date. What could have possibly possessed her? I mean, with Stefan and Booty sitting next to her, what would she want with Andrew?

"Yes, Mrs. Díaz?" He's so cute. And formal. And polite. I love him.

Huh? No, I didn't mean I love him like that, I meant, as in, he's so sweet. It's a wonderful thing that people can't read minds, and another blessed thing that Robi's not here at my mother's invitation.

"You should try the fondue with the seafood since you like fish so *mush*," Mami says.

Wow! That was pretty good English, as well as a thoughtful thing for her to suggest. "Yeah, Andrew, let's split that one. The platters are for two," I say.

"Actually, I don't eat seafood," he says. Mami nods and goes back to reading the menu. I guess she must not have heard him.

"But you go fishing with Iggy and his dad. And you don't like seafood?"

"Nope. I like fishing. I don't like eating fish."

"You're kidding."

He shakes his head.

"Man, you are one weird guy."

"Why?"

"Because! You live in Florida, and you don't like seafood. That's like a vegetarian living in Texas."

"Then I guess I'm weird. That would make you even weirder for going out with me."

The evening is pleasant, except for Maria the Waitress, who stops the chatter at our table whenever she comes by to refill our glasses. It's unfair that anyone can be so beautiful without trying. It's unfair that Booty and I are left drumming our fingers in her shadow. But not Mami. She looks great tonight, glowing over there, in a category all her own. *Miami Herald* headline reads: WOMAN WITH CANCER SHINES.

Stefan sees me noticing Mom and smiles at me all big-brotherly. I guess this whole cancer thing has taken off his edge. Good, he needed it.

Right after finishing the last stuffed mushroom, Andrew excuses himself to use the restroom. Too many water refills. Booty maneuvers her way out of the booth and over to Andrew's spot next to me.

"Hi," she says.

"Hi." Friendly girl. I can't for the life of me remember her name from when Stefan introduced us. I don't suppose she'd appreciate Booty.

"You know, I know your boyfriend from somewhere."

"Oh yeah?" Boyfriend. Cool.

"Yeah, I can't remember from where, though. Your brother says he goes to UM, so it can't be school. I go to FIU. *No sé.*"

"Maybe you know his friend Iggy?"

"Wait a minute! No, you know from where? He goes to my gym."

Gym? He never mentioned belonging to a gym, although I suppose he must, right? You can't get that lean by standing in the PE field all day. "Really?"

"Yes, that's definitely him. I didn't think he had a girl-friend."

"Well, we've only been going out for about a month."

"Oh, okay," she says, becoming real quiet. Maybe she's had her eye on him too. It's hard to miss Andrew. I remember how taken I was with him the first day, even when I thought I wouldn't like him. His presence is hard to ignore.

I watch Mami scoot past Dad with her purse in hand, excusing herself from the table. She looks at me for a moment and grins, probably pleased that Isa and Stefan's fiancée-to-be are getting along so well.

"You have highlights, right?" Stefan's date asks, squinting at my head. "They're hard to see in here."

I have no idea what she's talking about. I don't have highlights. Why would she think that? Maybe she's a hair colorist. "Probably from the sun," I say. "I've been in the pool a lot lately."

Andrew returns and stands next to us, waiting for his seat back. Stefan's girl takes the hint and gets up. "All right, I'll see you later. You're going, right? With us to the beach?" She quickly scans Andrew's physique.

"No, sorry. I can't get in yet."

"I can talk to my brother if you want. He can get you a good ID."

Isn't this lovely. "Thanks, but I'll just wait two more weeks till my birthday. Nice to meet you." Booty. Booty girl. Highlight-seeking girlfriend-wanna-be.

"Same here, Isa." She ambles off to the restroom. Everyone's going to the restroom.

"I've seen her somewhere," Andrew says, settling back in.

"She's seen you, too. You go to a gym?"

"Girelli's? Yeah, why?"

"Nothing. I just didn't know." I guess there's no reason for him to have ever brought it up. That's like bringing up in conversation that you go grocery shopping once a week. Duh.

"I go every day after work. You're right, that's where I've seen her."

Maria the Waitress returns with trays of dessert bites for dunking in chocolate fondue, one of which has a lit candle on it. She places it in front of my brother, and we all sing "Happy Birthday." Then, she lays a tray between Andrew and me and sets our chocolate to warm. Mmm. Too bad my parents are here, or else I'd be ditching these little spears and feeding Andrew chocolate-coated strawberries straight out of my hand.

As my dad finishes paying the bill, I walk out slowly, envisioning the food coma I'll be in later tonight when my head hits the pillow. Andrew stays a few steps behind me to talk to Booty. What *is* her name?

Mami comes up alongside, putting her arm around me. "*Hola, hija.*"

"Mami." I kiss her cheek.

"*¿Isa, dime por fín, cuántos años tiene ese muchacho?*"

So how old is that boy, she asks. Damn, what do I tell her? I can't lie.

Almost like she knows, she implores without waiting for my response, "*Mi vida, ten cuidado. Por favor, no te enredes.*"

"Shhh, Mami, remember he understands Spanish," I whisper. "Why are you asking me again not to get involved? I am being careful." *I haven't slept with him yet, have I?*

"Isa—"

"Before you say anything, remember that I'm not leaving anymore. I can stay with him if I like him."

"*Mi vida*, he's too old for you."

"What?" I look back to see how far behind Andrew is. He's

132

out of hearing range. "How do you know how old he is?"

She raises an eyebrow. I guess I should know better than to think my mom is stupid or blind.

"Mom, he's just a few years older. It's not like he's married with children or anything." Actually, I'm surprised she's not being more forceful with this issue. Maybe she's realizing she'll push me away, like she did with Carmen, so she's taking it easier on me.

"*Te pido que por favor lo pienses, hija.*"

"There's nothing to think about. Besides, I'll be eighteen *ya pronto.*"

"*Me parece que estoy oyendo a Carmencita.*"

"I'm not Carmen. I'm staying here with you, aren't I? Can't I at least date someone I really like in exchange?" Yes! Good move, Isa. Rationalization at its best.

She thinks about this, but I can tell she's holding back with the guy in question a mere ten feet behind. "*Hablamos despues,*" she says.

But for some reason, I can't hang this up and talk about it later. "What do you have against Andrew? Is it because of Robi? Do you want me to go back with him, is that it? Because I won't."

"Shhh, *baja la voz. Isa, ese niño.*" She pauses, voice filling with irritation. "*No tiene interés en tí.*"

"Oh, all right, Mom, Andrew's not interested in me. So then why is he here tonight, and why have we been seeing each other for nearly a month, if he's so *not* interested in me?"

"*¡Ay, Isa, por Dios! Trrrust me. ¡En vez de oir a tu mamá,* *siempre tienes que ser tan cabezona!*"

I'm hardheaded? Jeez. And I shouldn't even say anything back to her. It's not worth it in her condition. Very calmly, I say, "Okay, so now I'm stubborn? Because I don't see anything wrong with Andrew, except maybe that he's a few years older than you'd like him to be? Explain that, when Papi's ten years older than you."

Ha! Got her again.

She scoffs, because apparently I'm still not getting it. "Isa, when I went to the restroom, *lo ví hablando con la camarera.*"

It must be the blank look I'm giving Mami, because she opens her eyes wide and nods her head, as if saying, *See? You should listen to me; I'm your mother.*

I pull my earlobe. "So what? I saw him talking to the waitress, too. That doesn't mean he's up to no good. Please, Mom."

"*Está bien, hija.* Fine."

She's lost it. Yes, I guess there's always the possibility that he was flirting with the waitress, but I seriously doubt it. She probably started talking to him, and that's what Mami saw. Whatever. She can interpret it however she wants. "I'll ask him and see what he says. *¿Está bien?*"

This satisfies her for the moment, and I know how long Mami can argue a moot point. But then, "*Ese niño es una mosquita muerta,*" she says right before my father catches up with us, putting his arm around Mami's shoulders.

I wait by the door outside, as my parents walk to their car. I feel so damn torn. Mami may be crazy, but she's also usually right about people. Then again, she's not herself lately, so I don't know that I can trust her judgment.

Andrew meets up with me, pulling a toothpick out of his mouth long enough to kiss my cheek and say, "You look absolutely gorgeous tonight."

I smile. But quietly I think about him flirting with the waitress and soon I'm obsessing about the last thing my mom said—*That boy is playing you.*

Seventeen

For the rest of the weekend, Maria the Waitress wasn't mentioned again. But now it's Sunday evening, and the whole thing is still bothering me, so I call Andrew before he leaves for a softball game. I put the bracelet he gave me in my drawer.

"Hey, babe, what's up? I gotta get outta here or I'll be late."

"I'll be quick. Andrew, the other night at the restaurant, did you know our waitress or something?"

"Did I know her? Like personally? No, why?"

"Because my mom saw you talking to her when she went to use the restroom, so I was just wondering if maybe you knew her."

He laughs for a second. "No. I only stopped to ask if she'd bring out dessert with a candle for your brother."

"Oh." And how did Mami see this as flirting?

There's a long pause while Andrew waits for any other

dumb questions bred from dumb ideas. "Isa? Don't do that, sweetie."

"Do what?"

"Get sensitive about things. You know I'm crazy about you."

I let this sink in. Coach Andrew, the hottie with the mysterious look and beautiful smile, not to mention the billboard body, is crazy about me. I mean, I know I'm pretty, but I'm no Maria the Waitress. "Me too," I say.

"I'll call you after the game if you'll be up."

"Don't bother. I'm helping my mom around the house, then going straight to sleep."

"All right, then. Isa?"

"Yes?"

He blows me a kiss over the phone. "You're awesome, sweetheart."

That boy is playing you. Mami's words rush in to taunt me, but I push them aside. She's crazy. This is an established family fact. "So are you. I'll see you tomorrow morning."

I hang up and take the bracelet out of the drawer.

Later, I hear the vacuum cleaner running at the other end of the house. I go to tell Mami that I'll take care of it, but when I get there . . . lo and behold, I almost don't recognize him. Stefan, doing woman's work. My first instinct is to run and get the camera, but instead I decide to lean against the wall and bust his chops.

"What in God's name are you doing?"

He runs the cleaner back and forth over the same area of the living room, neglecting the corners and edges. "What does it look like? Mami needs the help."

"You dork. Mami has always needed the help."

"At least I'm doing something."

"Yes, and you look great with a Hoover. It matches your outfit." I spin and head toward my parents' room.

"Oh, you're *so* hilarious!" he shouts over the motor.

My mother is in bed, looking at an old photo album. I'm talking old. These photos are black and white, not from using Photoshop to get them that way, but because there wasn't color film when they were taken. They're pictures of family from Cuba, an album I've seen a couple of times. Most of them are Dad's. A couple are my mom's. They were smuggled in with family members who came after him.

"*¿Qué haces, Mami?*"

"*Aquí, mirando estas fotos.* Have you ever seen them?"

"Yes, a long time ago."

She flips to a page somewhere in the middle and pulls out a loose photo. "You've seen this one?" She hands it to me.

It's of a man and woman, arms around each other. Their clothes are from the fifties, sixties maybe. They stand on the wooden stoop of a beautiful white house with palm trees on either side. "Yeah, but it's been a while." I sit next to her.

She smiles sadly, caressing the photo with the tip of her finger. "*Son Mami y Papi.* One of the only pictures I have."

"I know." My grandparents. I loved this picture when I

was little. My grandmother's eyes are bright, squinting in the sun. Her smile is exactly the same as mine and my mother's, though she wore a darker lip color than either of us would ever use. My grandfather was tall, and stood perfectly straight in a white suit, cigar at his mouth, proud of his beautiful wife and home. "*Qué elegantes*. I wish I could've known them."

"Believe me, *hija*, so do I. You would have loved them. They would have loved you, too."

"I know you've said they couldn't leave Cuba because of the situation there, but how did they die? You never talk about it."

"I know, I didn't tell you everything. It's not the kind of story a little girl likes to hear."

"All you've said is that your dad died from a heart attack, and your mom from having lost him." It was something she told me when I was little, and I just accepted it. It sounded so romantic. I've spent years wondering if I could ever die from heartache like that.

"*Verdad*" is all she says.

I stare at the picture. They look like ghosts from a golden age of *cuba libres*, bongos, and Tropicana. Their smiles sparkle, telling us they're okay, wherever they are. I glance at my mother. There's something in her face, something painful; it's starting to hurt me. "*¿Qué pasa, Mami?*"

She takes a deep breath and exhales heavily. "*Ay, mi hija*. It was so long ago. On some days, like today, I can't even remember what they look like. So I take out this book and try to see their faces in my mind."

I nod, trying to imagine what that's like. I don't think I could ever forget my mother's face, no matter how much time passes after losing her. It was the first face I saw coming into this world; it'll be the last in my mind on my way out.

She goes on. *"Isa, no murieron así."*

Okay. I always felt there had to be more to that story. Everyone else managed to escape Fidel's regime, so why not my grandparents? "Then how *did* they die?"

She stares at the photo, without blinking, urging her brain to go back, to collect scattered pieces of memories. *"Ay, Isa,* I can't, *mi vida."* She shakes her head out of frustration.

"Mami? What is it?" I put my arm around her.

"Hija, it was so long ago. I was only fifteen, but I can still see it *como si fuera ayer."*

Every now and then, my mother remembers things about Cuba that she wants to share with us. The sugary sands of Varadero, a park swing, an ice-cream vendor. Always happy memories, the ones she has no problem retelling. But then there are the others—the ones that hurt too much to talk about.

Her face reflects something dark and tormented. In Spanish, she begins.

"Isa, I was sleeping when they came in. There was a lot of yelling. Their voices scared me, but I couldn't tell if I was dreaming or if it was real. When I sat up in bed, I saw them, holding their rifles. They went into my parents' room and dragged them out. One of them had my mother by the nightdress, and it tore as he was pulling her. Her shoulder was show-

ing, and I remember thinking that any moment, the dress would come right off of her. They screamed at my father as they beat him, accusing him of things I knew nothing about."

She drops her head and cries. She sobs until I can't take it anymore, and I start crying, too. I turn Mami's face up to search her eyes. "What happened? Did they kill them? Who's 'they'?"

"*El gobierno, hija.*"

"The government? Mami, you don't have to tell me this if you don't want to."

"*Yo sé, mi vida*, but I have to. I should've told you this years ago. Besides, we don't know what will happen to me."

"Stop that. You're not going anywhere."

She wipes her tears and leans back on her pillow, closing her eyes. "*They took them. They came in the night and just took my parents, Isabelita. I still remember my mother telling me to run to Tío Raul's house and stay with him until they returned. But they never did.*" She laughs a painful laugh. "*I'm still waiting for them.*"

"But what happened to them?"

"*I was told afterward that they went to separate prisons for sending information to the States. Codes, messages, plotting against Fidel's regime. I was told they would be released after some interrogation. I was told it would all be cleared up soon. And then I was told they were shot.*"

My hands fly to my mouth.

I'd always heard these stories told by other people's grandparents, the kind of stuff told over a game of dominoes, when

141

they think the kids aren't listening. But I never thought Mami would be telling it; that it happened to my own flesh and blood.

"*Firing squad*." Her face drops into her hands, and she cries. I can hardly stand to see her this way, so I look at the picture of my *abuelos* instead. Happy, smiling *abuelos*, never thinking for a moment that Cuba would come to this, that they'd be killed in their own country for having their own views. I focus on their eyes, which seem to stare back, speaking volumes to me of things I will never fully understand.

Mami takes my hand. "*Perdóname, hija, por no haberte dicho esto antes*."

"It's okay, Mami. I don't think I would've understood all that if you'd told me when I was little. I'm glad I didn't know. I probably would've had nightmares or something."

"*Sí*. You would have."

"Do Carmen and Stefan know?"

"*Carmen, sí*."

Maybe that's why Mami holds back sometimes. Maybe it's hard enough that she lost her parents and then Carmen went away. She's probably afraid of losing me, too.

"So, *Tío* Raul brought you here with him?"

"No, I lived with him for four years, but then I left to live with *Tía* Marta in Miami, who had come during the Peter Pan flights. *¿Tú sabes de eso?*" She looks at me.

"Yes, when all the kids came from Cuba without their parents, I know. I just didn't know she was a part of that."

She rubs her eyes. "*Sí*. And then *Tío* Raul joined us afterward. He had followed my mother's instructions to send me to Miami if anything were to ever happen. That's when I met your father."

"I know. *Abuelo* and *Abuela* were *Tía* Marta's neighbors. Dad used to cut the grass in his undershirt and wink at you. I've heard that part a million times."

She laughs gently. "*Sí. Tu papá era tan buen mozo.*"

It's good to see her smiling, remembering a younger Dad. This is all so weird. I know my mother's never been one to talk about her past, and I see why. But maybe if she'd told me this sooner, I could've comforted her, or at the very least, been a little nicer. It helps to know what someone's been through before you wonder why they act so crazy.

We sit there for a while, as Mami flips through the rest of the photos. I try to imagine what it'd be like if my parents were plucked from our home in the middle of the night. How would I feel, wondering where they were and if they're even alive? I try imagining the anguish, the lack of answers. I try to imagine myself newly arrived in America, living with my aunt, trying desperately to shut out a memory that will always haunt me. I try seeing myself in a new country, managing without my parents, wondering if I'd ever feel happy again.

I think I'd forever be looking back, hoping that maybe, just maybe, I'd see them one last time.

Eighteen

I finish the sign to the right side of the canvas—Lummus Park, Miami Beach. Then I stand back and take in the whole image.

She sits looking out at the ocean, her white linen shirt billowing around her. The storm overhead is ready to come down. The beach has emptied, no one there but her. Her and a nearby food cart, locked up, its owner nowhere in sight. She is ready for the rain, ready to bare her wounds, ready to forget. The water will cleanse her. She watches the waves as they peak and collapse, with quiet resignation. She knows she will never see them again.

I look outside. As the real clouds rumble closer, I think about everything that's happening—about Mami's surgery tomorrow, her story about my grandparents, Andrew, not going to college—even Robi. Why? Why is all this happening? Why can't life just be simple? Nothing has gone as planned, nothing. I don't know if I can take all this. But I have to. I don't have a choice.

I wipe tears away from my face. I think I understand this girl now. I think I'm ready to wrap this up. The clock on the art room wall says it's time to go home. Leaning forward, I finish it off in the left-hand corner. *Isa.*

Wiping my brushes and trashing the wax paper with the last of my blends, I hurry to beat the real rain waiting outside. I grab my bag, the painting by the edge, and leave the room. Andrew is gone. I told him I wanted to finish the painting. Susy's gone. We haven't talked for over a week. Jonathan's gone too. Only the cleaning lady is here, sweeping outside the main house. Behind her the door is still open. I say a quick hello to her, then peer inside.

The computers and lights are off. So quiet. Tiptoeing inside, I breathe in the silence of the room. To my left is the bulletin board with its mess of memos. Under the leaves of papers, I search for the bright blue one I saw a couple of weeks ago.

There it is—the flyer for the Cuba Expo art contest. I rip it off the board and tuck it into my bag.

The next day, Baptist Hospital reflects the orangey-peach light of the late afternoon sun. For once the rain has let up, and I am reminded of why Miami has a reputation for beauty. I have time to kill since Mom is in recovery. I can't see her for a while, so I'm under this gazebo by the lake. These ducks could care less that I'm whistling for their attention.

In the parking lot there's a guy walking around placing ads under windshield wipers. This is the first time I've ever seen one of them. You find the papers on your windshield but never see who puts them there—like magical elves that fix shoes at night. The dude approaches my father's Infiniti, and I see him leave his flyer under the wipers.

When he's safely out of sight, I go to the car and pull the ad out. Great, it's for a new Girelli's Gym, opening up in Kendall. *Now two locations! Join today!* I'd heard about this gym even before Andrew mentioned it. Stefan said it's a meat market and plans to enroll shortly. But it's also right by UM. Probably why Andrew goes there.

Sigh. Let's see what Dad's doing. Inside the hospital I weave my way around staff members, wheelchairs, and a multitude of visitors, who all seem to be strolling at half a mile an hour. A sense of mild claustrophobia chokes me. I reach the waiting room where I left Dad and Stefan, but now my father's by himself.

"Hey, Dad."

He looks up. "*¿Qué tal, hija? ¿Qué hiciste?*"

"Nothing. Just went down to the lake, walked around the parking lot, came back. It's a beautiful day."

He nods. His knee bounces up and down at high speed. My father's never this quiet.

"Dad? Mami's going to be okay." Still, I understand how he feels. This surgery just better have stopped the cancer from spreading.

His knee stops bouncing. "I know, *hija*. I know."

146

"*¿Y Stefan?*"

"He went to the cafeteria. *¿Por qué no te vas un ratico, anda, y te llamo cuando salga Mami?*"

I guess he's right. I should go somewhere. It'll be a while before I get to see her if she's in recovery and doesn't have a room yet. Plus it's almost dinnertime. But I didn't bring the truck. "I came with you, Dad."

Staring ahead, my father leans to one side, reaches into his pocket, and pulls out his keys. "*Toma.*" He hands them to me.

"You want me to bring you something to eat?"

"No, Stefan's got it. Here." He gives me his cell phone. "Just in case. I'll tell Stefan to call you when she's in a room."

"Maybe I shouldn't go."

"Isa, we're not going to see her for at least an hour. Go somewhere. Just be careful. *Hay tráfico a esta hora.*"

"I'll go opposite traffic. By the time I come back, it should be mostly gone. Bye, Daddy." I kiss his cheek. And I'm off again, through the halls, at the elevator, past the gift shop, and out the door. Ah, fresh air. What is it about hospitals?

My watch says 5:30. Probably could've gone to work today if I'd known the surgery would take this long, but Jonathan said to take the day off to be with Mom. I guess he isn't as bad as he sometimes seems.

I love the smell of my dad's G35, nice and leathery. It's cool that he's letting me drive it. Wait till Stefan finds out. Dad never lets Stefan drive his car. Let's see . . . where do I go? Dadeland Mall? Nah, let Stefan shop for me. Bookstore in the other direction. Nope, bumper to bumper. I know. I pull out the flyer from my pocket and find the address for the gym's Coral Gables location.

Driving through Coral Gables is like driving through a postcard, with its tree-lined streets, vibrant hues, and old-world architecture. I have to come out here one day and just paint, really capture the colors of this city that, according to Mami, looks a lot like old Havana. Maybe I'll do that for her next birthday.

I wonder if Andrew's at the gym already. I can't wait to surprise him. I'd like to think it would brighten his day. I know I would've loved it if he'd shown up at the hospital's gazebo.

I find the gym, but a parking spot is a different story. The place is packed. Luckily I find a metered space in front of a bridal store. Pulling up, I yank the brake and slide my shades over my eyes.

I get out, feeling the drastic difference between the A/C inside and the oven-hot temperature rising from the pavement. That's one thing I was really looking forward to about Michigan—a little cold weather after all this heat. There's a bench outside the bridal store with a view of the gym's front entrance. I'll wait there, 'cause I'd stand out if I went in with these jeans and a T-shirt.

I scan the street for Andrew's car. No white 4Runner anywhere. Then again, there's a full parking lot on the other side of the building. I'll keep my eye on the corner. If

Andrew left work at his usual time, he should be getting here right about now.

But I don't see him. Of all people, I see Susy coming up the sidewalk, chatting with another girl. Both of them in workout pants and barely there tops, all laced in the back like bikinis. So I guess everybody and their mothers go to this gym but me? Seems more like the place to be than the place to do squats.

Susy doesn't see me and enters in a rush. I wonder if she's always come here or if she learned that Andrew did and just joined. Because that would really piss me off, if she thinks for one second she can flirt with him when she knows I won't be watching.

Andrew's never mentioned her coming here. Come to think of it, Andrew never mentions anything, and that's partly my fault because I don't ask. Because I'm so wrapped up with the way I feel with him that I don't bother.

Mi vida, ten cuidado. Por favor, no te enredes, Mami's voice creeps up on me again. I swear I'm cursed. How do I turn her off when I don't feel like listening to warnings? Suddenly a morbid thought hits me. She's gone. She's died from a complication and her ghost is talking to me.

Coño, stop it, Isa. Everything's really getting to you. I pull out Dad's cell phone and dial Stefan.

He answers on the first ring. "Hello?"

"What's going on?" I keep my eye on the corner of the building.

"Dad?" Stefan asks.

"Isa, you dork."

"Duh, I was just playing with you."

"Is Mami okay?" I ask.

"The doctor just talked to Dad. She's doing great, no room yet."

A loud breath escapes me. "Thank God."

"Yeah, no shit. I'll call you when we can see her. Where are you?"

"I'm out driving. I'll be back in a little bit. Tell me when you know anything."

"Okay. Bye. Driving? Wait—"

I close the phone with a loud smack. Where's Andrew? Maybe he's already inside, and I just missed him. How can I find out without standing at the glass like a peeping idiot? Oh, who cares. I get up and walk to the gym's window, cupping my face at the glass to block the glare.

Inside is a madhouse. Tanned, hard bodies, glistening under neon lights. A few people are actually working out, lifting weights, running on the treadmills. Most are greeting and chatting. Apparently it's happy hour at Girelli's.

A spinning class is just getting started, and the instructor shouts even with a headset on. I can see Susy on one of the bicycles, her feet pedaling quickly to keep up with the booming music. She's crouched over the handlebars, her workout pants stretched down to reveal a thong and a tattoo right above her butt. I never knew she had one. A tattoo, not a butt. Of what, I can't really tell. Is that a flower? A sun?

Whatever it is, a second later a hand's covering it—a guy's

150

hand, at the small of her back, someone with nice arms kissing her cheek. In fact, those arms look a lot like . . . wait a minute. That's Andrew. What the hell?

Suddenly I feel a surge of whoop-ass course through me as I yank the gym door open and make a beeline for my so-called boyfriend.

The girl at the front desk calls me over. "Excuse me . . ."

"I'm just going to tell someone something, one second," I explain. "I'll be right out."

She lets me go, and I push past a guy who looks like the Michelin tire man, find the spinning class, and stop next to Andrew. "Why, hello there," I say charmingly, trying to control my breathing.

His eyes open wide. "Isa!"

Turning to Miss Ass Crack, I smile from ear to ear. "Hey, *chica*. Nice to see you."

"Hey, what're you doing here?" She huffs and puffs on her bike. Her dumb friend on the one next to her gives me a look for no reason.

"Oh, nothing. Thought I'd come and see Andrew while my mom recovers from surgery. It'll be a while before I get to see her." Under these lights, Susy's blond highlights stand out. I never noticed them at work.

I turn to Andrew again. "Hi, sweetie." *Definitely no kiss for you, dipshit.*

"How's your mom?" he asks, running a hand through his hair.

A nervous hand, perhaps? "She came out of it okay, but I

haven't seen her yet. Can we talk somewhere?"

"Yeah, sure." Andrew exchanges looks with Susy.

With Andrew behind me, I spin around and head to the front door, completely aware of many faces looking at me. I could never come to this gym. I already feel like I don't belong.

Outside I lean against the glass. "Can you tell me what that was about?"

"I'm sorry?" He raises his eyebrows.

"Susy. First, I didn't know she came here, and second, you were being awfully friendly with her."

"Isa, explain."

"Explain? You want me to explain? No, Andrew, I think maybe you should talk. Why is she here? And since when are you so chummy with her?"

"I'm not chummy with her. I was just saying hi. Can't I say hi?"

"Okay, look, there's saying hi, and then there's 'Hey baby, don't move, I'm trying to cop a feel.'"

"You know, you're really blowing this out of proportion. I didn't know you were the jealous type."

The jealous type? Well, maybe it wasn't in me till now. Seeing Andrew touch Susy like that just pissed me off. I don't think I would've cared if it was anyone else, but knowing her and her reputation . . . well, that changes things. "Look, I'm sorry, but I happen to know that Susy . . ." I pause.

"What? Tell me."

"Look, Susy does anybody. She goes from guy to guy, and

sex is one big party for her, so I'm just a little frustrated because I saw how you touched her. She probably enjoyed it. And the fact that you guys are here without me . . ."

"Hello? Isa? You're not making any sense. This is stupid. I've told you how I feel about you. Can't you feel it every time we're together?" He reaches for one of my crossed arms.

I don't say anything, tongue tucked into my cheek. I'm sorry, but if it looks like a duck, it's probably a freakin' duck, or however that goes. I look at him deeply, trying somehow to transmit all my feelings, without having to say anything. All right, let's do a little test. If he really cares for me, he'll see those feelings on my face. If he can't, then he doesn't.

Andrew stares, his eyes searching mine, reading, analyzing. Maybe I am being stupid. Maybe Mami's got me all paranoid.

I'm crazy for you, Andrew. You make me feel beautiful and so alive. . . . If you feel at all for me the way I do for you, then I need to see it . . . I need to know, so I have no reason to be jealous . . . is this getting through?

"I know what the problem is," he says softly. "We haven't talked much. That's my fault. I don't like talking about . . . things, but I know you probably need it."

Hey, not bad.

I let out a deep breath. "What are we doing?" I ask. "I mean, I know you told me 'one day at a time' on our first date, and I know you said you're crazy for me, but how far are we going? I know that sounds like an unfair question after only a month, but I have to know, Andrew. People are telling me things, and I just don't know who to listen to."

He sighs. "Listen to yourself."

Yeah, that's a good one. Has he ever heard his inner voice when he's got it bad for somebody? Not quite the voice of reason, is it? "Should we be doing this?"

"That's up to you. I know how I feel about you, but I haven't heard much from your end."

He's right. I haven't told him much, either. I guess I have to. I can't keep doubting and defending him, doubting and defending. I have to pick one and stick with it, and if I get hurt, well then, I'll cross that bridge when I get there.

"Andrew . . ." Sigh. "I've never felt about anybody the way I feel about you, not even Robi." Maybe I shouldn't have said that. Whatever, keep going. "All I think about is you. At night, I lie in bed, thinking about your eyes, your hands, your voice, your kiss, your everything. Do you understand me?"

He pulls me close. "Yes, I understand." He kisses me.

Screw everyone. I don't care if Andrew is bad for me. If something so bad can make me feel this good, then I guess I'm going to hell. But first . . . "Look at me and tell me there's nothing going on with Susy."

His eyes slice right through me, that wicked look that has made mush out of me since day one. He presses his forehead to mine. "There is nothing going on with Susy."

I want to believe him so badly. His eyes are killing me. Stop it, Andrew. Stop looking at me like that. God, I'm such a sap! I squeeze his hands. "Okay. I'm taking your word for it." I watch his face for a few seconds. What am I looking for?

Twitching? Some sign of a lie?

"Isa, I wanted to tell you something the other night, but I wasn't sure how you'd feel about it."

Okay. I just look at him, waiting.

"I'm falling for you pretty hard. Harder than anyone in a long time. In fact, I think I . . . no. I'm sure I love you." His eyes watch mine intensely.

He didn't. Did he? Did he just say that? "That's funny. I thought the same thing too. At the restaurant." I lean my head on his shoulder and breathe into his neck. Just say it. Say it, Isa. "I love you, too."

He squeezes me hard.

"I gotta go," I tell him. "My mom's waiting."

"All right. Send her my best."

"I will."

After one last kiss I start toward the car, but he pulls me toward him again. "Isa, I was thinking about your birthday coming up, and . . . well, I want to do something nice. It's on a weekday, but maybe the following Saturday?"

"Like what?"

He looks down, scuffing the sidewalk with his sneaker, then looks back up. "Like go somewhere special, just the two of us."

I see.

"Of course, it's totally up to you, but I was thinking maybe . . ."

Please say it. No, don't say it. Okay, please say it.

"A room somewhere nice. The Biltmore? Let's really celebrate. Want to?"

Yes!

"Of course, Coach," I say, reaching around his shoulders and pressing my body against his. The thought of having Andrew all to myself will fuel many dreams tonight. "That would be so wonderful."

He hugs me tight and whispers, "I think it's what we both need."

"Need is right," I say, tugging on my earlobe.

Inside her hospital room, my mom looks okay. Tired, drugged, worn, but okay. I just want her to get better already so she can get out of here.

"*Jugo*," Mom whispers, eyes closed.

"Juice?" I repeat like a dork, since I heard her just fine the first time. "I'll tell the nurse, Mami." I ease my hand out of hers gently and tiptoe to the corridor to find whoever is assigned to my mother.

The nurse is one step ahead of me. Thin and dark-skinned, she strolls up with a small container of apple juice and brushes past me. "*Señora Díaz, un poco de jugo*," she says in an accent, Jamaican maybe, a hint of a smile at her lips.

"*Ay, gracias*." Mami takes the juice and tries peeling back the foil lid.

The nurse helps her. "Take small amounts so you don't get nauseated. Remember your anesthesia is wearing off."

I watch, feeling very powerless, as she takes a small sip. She looks so frail, so unlike her. After everything she's done for me in my seventeen years, I can't do anything for her now.

Except be here with her. That's it.

The nurse leaves, and I reclaim my spot next to Mami, taking her hand. "Hi."

She breathes a quiet laugh and closes her eyes again. "Hi, *mi vida*."

Her IV drips. Slowly. I hesitate, then, "I love you."

With hardly any strength, she squeezes my hand and dozes off.

I know she knows. But still . . . I had to say it.

Nineteen

Four days away, my birthday's been giving me a lot to think about. It's been hard to concentrate on anything else. At least I've been distracted a little with my mom's postsurgery care. The first couple of nights were rough for her with high fevers and some pain, but the Percocet's been taking care of that.

Now she's doing a lot better and is itching to get out of the house. I've got just the thing for her. With Andrew fishing again, it's the perfect day to spend with my family. We've all been home a lot since her operation, and now's a good chance to show her how much she means to me.

"Are you ready?" I ask, peering into her room.

She slips a loose-fitting shirt over her head and fluffs her hair. "*Sí, ya. ¿A dónde vamos?*"

"You'll see. We'll get there soon enough."

Dad, Stefan, Mom, and I get comfortable in Dad's car, and

there's a real sense of excitement we haven't felt in a while. Since Stefan and I are usually out doing something else, it's been a long time since we hung out as a family. I really miss Carmen today.

My dad drives to the Coconut Grove Convention Center. Mami starts bouncing in her seat because she knows where we're headed. When we get there, we pay the parking fee and find a good spot close to the entrance.

"Isa," my mom says, "qué bueno que decidiste venir este año. Yo sé que te va a encantar."

"I know, Mami. That's why I'm here. I know I'll like it." Some might say I've come to the Cuba Expo this year to please my mom after the surgery. But that's not why, not really. This is the first time I want to. The story she told me has opened up something in me. I realize there's a whole vault of stories to hear, a whole world of things to understand about who I am. Without them, I can't possibly know where I'm going.

We pay at the entrance and present our tickets. Inside, a band plays *salsa* music. Stefan is already dancing before he passes the turnstile. A group of professional dancers graces the stage, while on the floor, the crowd watches them and dances along. Dad takes Mami's hand and spins her around slowly. Their feet mirror each other with precise steps. Then he tries dipping her, and she refuses with a laugh.

To our right is a giant map of Cuba and the surrounding waters. People are placing pushpins into the spots where they're from. Mami takes one and tacks it right along with hundreds of others from Havana. My father pushes one into Santiago de Cuba. I know this seems really weird, but I want to place a pin, too, except Miami's not there. Stefan and I look at each other. He rings his arm around me.

After that we stroll the vendors' section of the convention. Everything Cuban you could possibly imagine—from cigars to traditional *guayaberas*, photographs to photo CDs, books to DVDs—all about Cuba, all about culture. Mami buys a little doll, dressed in a traditional folk dress, its hair rolled into a shiny, brown bun at the side of its head. Usually I might see this in a store and think, *God, how tacky*, but today it looks beautiful.

I can't stop thinking about the other end of the expo. The end where artisans have taken shop to display their crafts; the end where an art exhibit will boast its winners. It's making me really nervous, because Mami knows nothing about what's there. I hope it's there. I *did* turn it in on time.

We stop at a food court set up in the back where it's loudest. Nothing like a good spread of Cuban delicacies to stir up people's emotions, get them talking about their memories. Mami and Dad have plates of *carne de puerco, congrí, maduros*, and *yuca*. Staples in Cuban cuisine—shredded pork, rice and beans, fried plantains—the best stuff on Earth, especially with that *mojo* sauce. I'm splitting a *ropa vieja* with Stefan—shredded, saucy beef piled over a huge mound of rice. That and a flan. It's all good, but it's definitely not Mami's.

"*¿Mami, quieres un pedacito de flan?*" I offer her a bite.

"*No, mi vida, gracias*. I don't want to know if it's better than mine." She laughs.

"*Ay*, Mami, that Key lime pie was not better than yours. Robi didn't know what he was talking about."

She shrugs. "Have you talked to him again, *hija*?"

"No. He hates me."

"I doubt that, *mi amor*. He loved you."

"I know, Mom. I know." I'm going to leave it right there this time.

"*Déjala*," my father interjects. Whether he's talking to me or my mom doesn't matter. I guess we both need to get off each other's back.

My mom lets it go. She smiles and folds her hands under her chin. "*Qué bueno es tener mis hijos aquí conmigo.*" She stares at the bubbles in her soda. "I wish Carmen was here."

"Me too," I say.

"Me too," says Stefan.

My father kisses my mom's hair and leans back to stretch. His seat screeches as his arms extend, then his weight takes the bad end of the balance. He tips backward, his feet kicking the underside of the table, making the grains of rice jump on the plates, as his chair and body slam onto the floor.

"*¡Coño!*" flies out of his mouth as he hits. Then he's laughing, that wheezy, breezy laugh that always gets me. At other tables, people clap and cheer as Dad quickly scrambles to his feet and takes a bow.

"Hey, Dad, I didn't know you were part of the entertainment this year." Stefan laughs. "Embarrassed?"

"*Me importa tres pepinos,*" Dad says.

How would I translate that for Andrew? *I don't care three cucumbers?* Whatever, it's way funnier in Spanish anyway.

My stomach starts hurting. Not because of anything I ate, but because we are now slowly heading for the art exhibits. Mami stops at the first set of tables and partitions, and at the second, and at the third. She's enjoying them all, but I wonder if she's looking for something in particular, something that really speaks to her.

Around the corner, we come face-to-face with a long wall covered in canvases. Ribbons of blue, red, and white dot some of the paintings. There are sections labeled senior contestants, adults, teens, and children under twelve. We start at the senior end and work our way down. I quickly scan the entire collection and spot it. My beach girl. I look away and wait for Mami to gravitate toward it.

She speaks to me over her shoulder. "*Ay,* Isa, anything of yours could easily be here, *mi vida.*"

I say nothing. I just nod. My stomach flips again. Dad is ahead of her, admiring the adult entries. He stops to look at one of a mountainside covered in palm trees. He takes a handkerchief from his pocket and dabs his eyes.

Stefan stands next to me and leans his head on mine. He whispers, "Isa, why don't you paint something Cuban for Mami? Of all the paintings you've made, nothing Hispanic. *Acomplejada.*" There's that complex thing again.

"Be quiet, Stef. I'm not *acomplejada.* I'm ahead of the game."

He gives me a quizzical look.

"Just wait," I say. "We're almost there."

He raises his chin and quickly scans for a familiar name among the paintings.

"*Qué bonitos son todos*," Mami says. She's right, they're all really good. I probably didn't even come close. I probably got one of those honorable mention thingies.

We cross from the adult panel into the teen section. I guess it's a good thing that I'm not eighteen, or they would've placed my painting with all these adult ones. But that gives me an edge in the 13–17 category, doesn't it? I can see it. She hasn't seen it yet, but Dad's almost there. It's got a white ribbon. Third place. I'll take it, considering I didn't enter it for a ribbon anyway.

Mami's standing next to it. I watch her carefully to see if she notices, if it stands out to her. Then her gaze falls on my painting, feet pausing. She could see my name in the bottom corner if she wanted to, but she doesn't. She's focused on the girl—the girl watching the water, gazing down the shore, oblivious to the winds and clouds around her. The girl facing the motherland, hoping her parents might emerge from the sea, come to join her and tell her not to be afraid, that everything will be okay, but they won't. And she knows they won't.

Her face changes from pale to pink. Her hand covers her mouth, her lower lashes glisten. My father stands with her to see. He spots my name, then looks at me. Does he understand? Does he see the connection? Of course he does. He has to.

My heart is beating so fast, I can hardly take it. Have I upset her? Have I forced her to see something she's been avoiding? So she's a *cubanita* at heart. So she'll always be yearning for home. So what? That's who she is.

She finally sees my name, and a low groan escapes her as she cries quietly against my father's shoulder. "*Yo lo sabía.* I've never seen a painting like this in all the years I've been coming here. This tells more than all of these." She gestures to the length of the exhibit. "It had to be yours, *hija.*"

She grabs my hand, and I suddenly feel very lucky to have her. To have them all, even Carmen somewhere out there. She kisses my hand.

"Mami, I just want you to know something, though."

"*¿Qué, mi vida?*"

"Home is anywhere, okay? You don't need to be searching for anything. Even your mom and dad are here, too. Cuba's just a place. It's nothing without you, without us."

She smiles in a way I haven't seen before. It's proud, but it's also something else. It's connection, it's understanding. It's . . . *finally, my daughter makes a decent attempt to understand me.* She hugs me and kisses my cheeks, over and over, caressing my hair, making a spectacle in front of the folks around us.

"Uh . . . Mami, people are watching."

She kisses my cheeks ten more times. "*Me importa tres pepinos.*" The three cucumbers again. I can't explain it. It's a Cuban thing.

Twenty

My birthday came and went. I'm officially an adult now, though it sucks it had to happen on a Tuesday. All the presents, flowers, and kisses were cool, but the real partying starts this weekend—the big weekend.

I dance around my room while on the phone with Andrew. "Do you have to go fishing tonight? Won't you be tired tomorrow? That would suck, you know." I spin the bracelet on my wrist over and over, imagining Coach stripping down to *nada*.

"Check in's at one o'clock, but we won't be going till night, right? So I'll be fine. What are you telling your mom?" he asks.

"That we're going out to dinner and maybe hitting some clubs afterward."

"Don't worry. I'll be ready. What're you doing tonight?" he asks.

"Nothing. Staying home."

"Aw, *pobrecita*, poor baby. How's your mom doing?"

"She's better. Already started her radiation therapy."

"Can she go out?"

"Yeah, for sure."

"Why don't you take her to the movies or something?" he suggests.

"There's an idea. Maybe I'll do that."

"Good little *cubanita*," he says with a chuckle.

My mouth opens to protest, but something stops me. Probably the fact that it really doesn't bother me anymore. So I'm a *cubanita*, too. So I do things for my mom. So what?

"All right, Coach. Catch a big one. Maybe we'll grill it here on Sunday, if you want. You should hang out with my parents more, so they can get to know you."

"Definitely, sweetie. I'll call you tomorrow. Have fun."

"You too."

We hang up, and I plop into my desk chair. I start a new e-mail:

From: Isabel E. Díaz
To: C. Díaz-Sanders
Subject: Big Night

Carmen, how've you been? Thanks for the money and the dress. It fits perfectly.

Guess what? Andrew and I are taking a big step tomorrow. Please don't tell anybody. Mami would kill me. Dad would start his lecture about responsible sex. Stefan would beat Andrew's ass. Nobody seems to like him, even though he's nice to me. I'm sending you a picture. He's sooo hot, which can suck, since other girls flirt with him a lot. Mami says he's not interested in me, but I just don't see it. If he's not, then he's a really good actor. Say hi to Dan for me.

Love, Isabel

I attach a photo of Andrew and me, heads together at Stefan's birthday dinner, smiling, then hit "Send." There's a knock at my door, and cologne filters in, which could only mean one person.

"Open."

Stefan turns the knob and peeks in. "What're you doing?"

"Looking for movie times."

"For what?"

"I'm going to see if Mami wants to go. If not, I'll go alone. I don't care."

"You've gotta be kidding me. Isa, *mama*, you're eighteen! Let's go, come on. We'll go to that new place that just opened in the Grove—the Library, I think it's called."

"Nah, it's okay," I say, but Stefan walks in and opens my closet.

"No, Isa. You're coming with me. I've been waiting all this time to take my little sis out partying, so find something hot. What is this?" He pulls out a flowery dress with a tag still attached.

"Carmen sent it. For my birthday."

"Figures." He reracks it and continues to search.

"What time are we coming home?" I ask. I don't want to be out too late partying.

"Isa, who cares? What, do you have an appointment with the Catholic Church in the morning? Come on, get up. Up!" he orders.

"Fine." I guess it would be fun. I'm just not much of a partier. I've seen what clubs have done to Stefan's brain. I get up and push him out of my way. "What's the place like?"

"Casual. Wear jeans or something. I'm leaving in half an hour to pick up Maite."

"Who?"

"My girlfriend?" he says.

"The one at the restaurant on your birthday?"

"Yes."

So that's her name! "Wow. A record for you, eh, Stefan?"

"Very funny. She's a sweetheart. I think I'll keep her."

I'm too stunned to speak. My brother's in love? *Ñoooo.* Unbelievable.

Half an hour later I pass my parents in the living room on my way out. "Bye, I'm going out with Stefan."

"*¿A dónde van?*" Mami asks, her eyes glued to Univision.

"To the Library."

"*¿Sí? Ay*, how nice."

Behind the *TV Guide* my father chuckles quietly.

The Library is the coolest place I've ever seen. It's wall-to-wall fake books, globes, and dark leather couches. The place is jam-packed with people, half of whom are wearing over-twenty-one wristbands, holding their drinks high above them as they try to navigate through the crowd. The music is awesome, a power mix of everything any decent partier would care to listen to. The center of the huge room has a dance pit, and the people inside bounce in unison under the colored lights. I think I'm in love.

I used to wonder what people saw in dance clubs, whenever I watched *Wild On!* on the E! channel. They always looked so happy, *woohoo*ing for no reason, drunk beyond comprehension. But I think I get it now. There's a strong vibe here. Everyone's gathered for the same reasons—to have a good time, to escape. I can see how someone could get hooked on this.

I guess my outfit worked, because guys are staring. I'm getting hi's left and right. This must be how Andrew feels when girls go gaga over him.

Andrew. *Ay, ay, ay.* Tomorrow is it. I probably won't sleep tonight. I just know we'll have a great time. I hope I'm not too nervous to relax, because I must relax. It's the only way to go. And at the Biltmore, too, of all places. It'll be wonderful and romantic and memorable, and . . .

"Isa, you want something virgin?" My brother shouts over my brain fog.

"Huh?"

"Virgin daiquiri, virgin margarita, virgin Coke?" He laughs.

"Oh." Duh. "Get me a Diet."

He turns back to the bartender. I glance around, taking in

the scene. A great Nine Inch Nails song comes on, which I always forget the name of, but the lyrics are deliciously bad. The dance floor is going crazy. I'd say this song just elevated everyone to a higher plane of partyhood.

Next to me, Maite squeals in delight, then wraps her arms around Stefan's waist. Across from me a guy and a girl hammer down two shots of whatever, then proceed to swallow each other's faces. They don't care that anybody's watching; they're enjoying their performance. They need a room, far, far away from here.

I know I came with these two goons, and I'm surrounded by hundreds of people, but all of a sudden, I feel alone. Everybody seems to have someone to share this song with. Except for a shitload of guys with their backs to the wall, watching the rest of the room climb to musical ecstasy. Why did Andrew have to go fishing?

Suddenly the place comes together in a deafening cry that sends a shiver up my spine. The crowd shouts the lyrics with glee.

Holy shit. A room full of drunk, horny people. This is making me dizzy. Stefan is grinding his hips into Maite's, with his drink in one hand and my Diet Coke in the other.

"Here, give me that," I say, taking the glass from him. "Before you spill it on me." The music bangs my brain, the lyrics feed my fantasies of Andrew. I can just see him now . . . pounding like the rhythm in this club. This is driving me insane. Tomorrow is too far away.

Then there's a face next to me, a hottie of unspeakable

beauty with green eyes. "Wanna dance?" he asks.

Uh. I shouldn't. I know I shouldn't. Not to this song, anyway. "No, thanks."

"You sure?" He tilts his head, giving me one last chance before he's off to ask someone else.

I could transfer my thoughts of Coach onto this guy. I could, but I won't. "Yeah, I'm sure. Thanks, though."

He shrugs and spins off into the sea of people. I feel bad for having turned him down, but after giving Andrew a hard time for having his hand so close to Susy's butt, I'd be a hypocrite if I grinded with this guy.

"What did he say?" Maite yells into my ear. She's already buzzed and doesn't know I can hear just fine.

"He asked me to dance."

"Why didn't you?"

"My sister's a good girl," Stefan shouts, before I can conjure up an answer of my own.

My sister's a good girl. That sounds like an insult. Is he saying I don't know how to have fun? Is he saying I don't know how to let go? Is that how people see me? Well, nobody's seen me with Andrew, but Andrew knows. And he'll know me even better tomorrow.

The song extends for another few minutes. The DJ's not stupid. He knows which tunes to keep and which to let go. It's a miracle that people are not leaving to work off the sexual tension from this song. It's almost thick enough to see.

But by the time the song mixes flawlessly into a new one, I can spot the couples who've had enough, the ones ready to leave and indulge in more than music. One of them is a guy tall enough to play basketball leading a tiny girl by the hand, tugging her along like a prize. I wonder if they just met or came here together. Another couple could easily be mistaken for Carmen and Dan, were I not absolutely sure they're in Virginia, and that Carmen would never be caught dead at a club playing "Closer."

That's the name of the song!

And then I see another couple. They move in the shadowy part of the room, away from the dance floor and smoke machines. They're kissing like there's no tomorrow, her hands tousling his hair, his strong jaw commanding hers. Commanding hers. My heart stops.

Wait. I know that jaw. That hair.

The dance scene fades from my vision, and the music plays in the far distance, as if from another place.

"Isa? Watch your drink, *mama*."

Watch your drink, I think I heard my brother say. *Watch your drink? Watch your man*, my brain whispers. *Watch your man devour someone else.* I hear a grinding noise in my head—my teeth. My stomach flips as I stand there with my drink dripping off the edge of the glass. My brother straightens it.

That can't be Andrew. He's out fishing with Iggy and his dad. *It's not him, Isa. He wouldn't do that to you. He said he was crazy about you, remember? He wouldn't . . . it can't be!* There's no way.

But it *is* him. There's no mistaking those eyes, that look.

172

They pull apart, and under a beam of red light, I see the girl's face way too clearly. Susy, grinning, biting her lower lip. I feel completely drained of blood. My feet are planted into the ground, and all I can do is watch. Watch, as he runs his hands along her shoulders, back, down to her ass. Watch, as she presses her tits into his chest, like I've done so many times. Watch, as he whispers into her ear, and they make for the door faster than you can say *fuck me.*

"Isa?" My brother's in my face.

Shut up, Stefan! Shut the hell up! But I can't say it. Every inch of me is paralyzed. My heart is going to break out of my chest any second now. I watch as he leads her out the door until they're out of sight.

Ese niño es una mosquita muerta. He's not interested in you.

How could I have been so stupid? So blind?

It's a need, hija, the power of need.

"Isa?" Stefan's arms are around me, Maite is at my side, lightly touching my waist. *"¿Qué pasa, mama?"*

I want to tell him I'm floating through a tunnel with no air. I want to tell him he was right about Andrew. But the laser lights and the smoke and the music all swirl together like a nightmarish carnival. The party people dance and howl, their laughter, multiplied in my head, over and over again.

"Just get me out of here."

Twenty-one

"Stefan, I am *not* going to plow a service truck into the side of Andrew's car." I open my night table drawer and begin looking for the right color nail polish for tonight's momentous occasion.

Stefan grabs the bracelet Andrew gave me off my dresser and hurls it into the trash. "No? Then I will."

"Would you stop it?" I swear, this big brother thing is getting to be too much.

"I told you. I told you you couldn't trust that dickhead."

"No, you didn't. Stef, would you calm down?"

He paces in the middle of my room. "I'm gonna kick his ass all the way back to Indianapolis."

"Daytona."

"Whatever." He throws himself on my bed, tossing and

retossing my pillow into the air. "Even Maite knew it. She saw how he was with Susy at the gym, but didn't say anything because she wasn't sure. It might've just been innocent flirting."

"There's no such thing, Stefan. Flirting is cheating's ugly cousin."

"What?"

"Never mind. Look, I'm going to handle this, not you. It's my problem."

"You sure? 'Cause if you want, I can see to it that his tires go flat."

"Would you stop it?" I say, turning to look him in the eye. "I'm not going to do anything like that. In fact, I'm going to pretend nothing happened." I pick a bottle of nail polish and close the drawer. "After all, I'm not supposed to know his little secret, right? We're supposed to have a wild time tonight in a romantic hotel, aren't we? Celebrate our newfound love for each other?"

"Pfft," Stefan says, then gets real quiet.

Oh, yes. We'll celebrate all right.

Stefan and I lie there on the bed without talking for, like, ten minutes. Which is good. I can finally think without him going nuts around me. I'm a good girl, right? So I should probably take this with a grain of salt. I mean, Susy's just offering her slutty self, whereas Andrew told me he loved me.

"Turn my cheek, that's what I'm going to do. Give him a piece of my ass, just like he wants. What do you think about that, Stef?"

I look over. Stefan's asleep. For such a big goon, he can be pretty cute sometimes. I kiss his forehead. Then I lean back into my pillow and paint my toenails Bad Girl Red.

At the Biltmore Hotel Andrew and I order dinner in a courtyard restaurant. There's an accordion and violin duet playing. The night is so pretty.

"So how was fishing last night?" I ask, chin in my hands, elbows on the table.

His eyes turn to the fountain next to us. "Awesome!"

"Yeah? That's so great that you and Iggy go fishing every weekend like that. You guys must be really good buddies."

"Uh-huh, he's really cool. Super guy." He slides the silverware out of position, into position, out of position . . .

"Right." I nod. *Right, asshole.* "So tell me again, if you and Ig are such good friends, why'd you move out? I think you told me, but I must've forgotten."

"I said I wanted a place of my own, which is true, but also because Iggy . . . well, he's great and all, but the dude gets jealous, you know? He got some dumb idea that I was after all his girlfriends."

Ohhhhh. I see it now. Clearly. You guys are not good buddies *anymore.* You don't even talk to each other since you started taking away all of Iggy's girls with your charm and your looks. And then came Iggy's last girl, Susy.

Son of a bitch.

"Man, that *is* dumb!" I laugh, sitting back in my chair, fake-wondering how anybody could think that of Andrew. "Is that why he never introduced you to Susy when they were going out?"

"I guess so. I never met her till day camp at Anhinga started. I never even knew she was *the* Susy he talked about."

Riiight, and that's when your radar zeroed in on her bull's-eyed butt and my stupid heart. My stupid, stupid heart.

"Interesting. And wasn't it also a coincidence that the two of you ended up in the same gym? Small world, isn't it?"

"Yep. Small world." Andrew chugs his water.

Our drinks come—a beer, a Diet Coke, and a shot of something. After the waiter leaves, Andrew picks up the shot glass. "For my little *señorita*, on her eighteenth birthday!" He leans in for a kiss first, before handing it to me, and I can't help but think of where his lips were last night. My insides get all tight, no butterflies in sight, but I go along with it.

"Thank you. To a wonderful evening." I take the shot glass from him. I'm gonna need it.

"To a wonderful evening," he says back, with a wicked smile that might've induced some form of swooning, were I not so ludicrously pissed right now.

I place the glass to my lips and shoot back the fiery liquid. Damn! I place it back down with a hard clank.

"Wow!" Andrew says, readjusting his seat, mouth open. "That's my girl!"

I smile. Yep, I'm gonna get buzzed and you're gonna get it all right. Good girl, my ass. "So where's our room?"

"Eleventh floor." He reaches across the table for my hand. "With a balcony. View of the golf course and all of Coral Gables."

"Really?" I knew that already when I called the hotel. All the better. "That's so sweet of you, Andrew."

Our plates arrive, and I make it a point to enjoy the lobster tail as much as possible. Thank God my bloodstream now has some fuel to battle the Goldschlager that's racing through it.

After we finish, the waiter brings a dessert menu, but Andrew waves it away, requesting the bill instead. Interesting, we always have dessert. The waiter returns, and Andrew signs the check.

"Know what I think?" Andrew asks, folding the receipt and placing it in his wallet.

That you're the hottest shit ever to blow through here?

"No, tell me."

"I think we should have dessert in our room." He watches my eyes carefully and waits.

"I think that's a great idea. It's about time we really celebrate." I bite my lower lip and softly bat my lashes. Hook, line . . .

"Let's go, then."

Sinker.

The elevator rattles, its little bells ding softly. The doors open to a Mexican tiled foyer and carpeted hallway ahead. I've never been inside the Biltmore, but I know it has a reputation for being haunted. Maybe the ghosts are following us right now. Maybe they're reading my thoughts. Maybe their presence will give me more strength.

We reach the room, where Andrew pauses before slipping in the card key. "I just want you to know . . . this summer has been the most awesome ever because of you. You're the most incredible person. All I want is for you to have a great time."

Blah, blah, quit jerking me around. "I'm sure I will, Andrew." I'm sure I will.

He pops open the door and flicks on the light. For a moment I almost forget why I'm here. Andrew's dad will freak when he sees the Amex bill. Roses everywhere, a basket of blank canvases and new oils wrapped in cellophane and a red bow, and in the corner of the room—the painting of the *guajiro* we saw on our first date.

Good move, jerk.

I fight back the urge to cry and tell him it's okay, that I forgive everything. Let's just go on as if nothing ever happened. You really are a wonderful person, you just got caught up in Susy's web, I understand. My hand covers my mouth. Why did he have to buy that painting?

"Well?"

"It's wonderful, Andrew. Really, it is." I don't believe this. Why would he go through so much trouble just to screw me over? Have I been that hard to win? "It's just . . ."

"Just what?" His expression dampens. Hurt maybe?

No, Isa, don't do it! Don't tell him you saw him. He's been lying to you, remember? He's been playing you like a wide receiver in fantasy football. When he gets tired of you, he'll trade you away for someone who'll rack in more points.

God, this sucks! How did I let him play me like that? I lace my arms around his neck.

"It's just . . . I can't believe you bought me that painting. You are too sweet! God, I love you!" There you go. Good girl. Play him back.

He tries to kiss me, but I turn my cheek, offering my neck instead. "I knew you'd like it." He breathes into my skin, holding me close.

I don't think I can take much more of this, but I have to. If I want to go through with it, I'll have to get him right where I want him.

He leads me into the suite, showing me the gifts and some chocolate-covered strawberries on a table. I remember at Stefan's birthday how I would've loved to have fed him those strawberries had my parents not been around to watch. I could've easily given in to him that night. But I didn't, thank God.

"Ah, so there's dessert." I pick up a strawberry and touch his bottom lip with it. His mouth opens, but I pull it back and take a bite with a smile.

"That's okay," he says, drawing an imaginary line from my chin down to the hollow of my neck, "that's not dessert anyway."

"It's not? What is?" Mr. I-Love-Myself.

"This."

He pulls me into his kiss, and totally against my will, the butterflies return. Which kills me. Fine, they can stay, but this is the last time I'll let them in for Andrew Corbin. I can't believe he's doing this to me. I can't believe I fell for his act. I should've known I couldn't trust him on our first date, when he faked me out with his mom being dead.

"What's the matter?" he asks, swiping my lashes with his thumb.

I'm crying? That's just great. *Push it aside, Isa. He's an asshole.* Yeah, but an asshole I fell for, an asshole I thought loved me. Wouldn't Robi love to know he was right? "Nothing. I'm just so happy."

I'm just so pissed it'll have to end this way.

He wants to kiss me again, but I pull away. I walk over to the balcony curtains, slide them aside, and open the doors. I turn off the outside light to see better. Our room is in the shadows, away from the pool. There are two chairs and a little table out here. The sky is void of stars. The city, alive with lights. "Andrew?"

"Babe?"

"You know how much I've been thinking about you all week?"

"Believe me, I know." He sits on the couch's armrest. "I've been thinking of you, too."

"No, I don't think you do. I'm dying here, dying to get this going already. Seriously. I don't want to waste any more time."

"I hear you." He falls back onto the couch and stretches out.

"No, don't lie down. Can you please turn off the lights? I want to do it out here. On the balcony."

He smiles like the devil he is and springs from the couch in two seconds flat. "You totally read my mind." He bolts for the switch. "Is it dark enough? Wouldn't want anyone to see us."

"Yes, it's completely dark out here. There's nobody. Just a few people sitting on the golf course."

Then Andrew is behind me, wrapping his arms around my waist, kissing my ear and neck.

"Another thing," I say, leaning back into his arms, trying real hard to seem like I'm enjoying his willing body pressed against me. "I know this sounds crazy, but . . . well, it's kind of embarrassing."

"What is? Don't be embarrassed by anything, sweetie. I'll do whatever you want. This night's all for you."

You couldn't be more right about that. "I kind of have this fantasy—"

He presses harder. "I'm liking it already."

"Where I come out here and find you ready for me. Could we do it like that?"

"Anything you want. That sounds sexy as hell."

"Okay, then wait for me in the chair. The less you're wearing, the better."

His laugh is low and mischievous. It's no wonder he enjoys games, being a playa' himself. "Yes, ma'am. Woohoo!"

"Woohoo!" I twirl a finger and disappear into the bathroom. And there I wait against the door, watching myself in the mirror, feeling my heart beginning to pound. My palms sweating, my fingers at my earlobe. Honestly, I don't know whether or not I'm doing the right thing, but I don't care anymore. For my sanity, and to make sure I don't think of him ever again, I've gotta do it.

I start peeling off my dress.

Quietly I click off the bathroom light and crack open the door. The lights are off, but, faintly, I see something rustling in the darkness of the balcony. My eyes adjust a bit, and I can see the comforter's gone from the bed. He's outside, waiting. I drop my dress on the floor and wrap a towel tightly against my chest.

My heartbeat's in my throat. My blood pounds against my eardrum as I cross the room and stand by the wide open doors. *Come on, Isa, you can do it.* Deep breath, then I float into his view, gripping the bathroom towel tighter.

From the chair, he whistles, solid chest and legs uncovered by the comforter draped across his lap. On the little table, a condom packet. "Hey, there."

My lips are trembling, but I manage a smile.

"How's this?" he asks.

I stroll up and kiss him. "Perfect. But it'd be even more perfect without this." I step back, sliding the comforter off of him, tossing it into the room. Nice. Very nice, Coach.

His knee bounces up and down, as he looks around. "You're a fierce one." He laughs, eyeing my towel. "Your turn."

"A fierce one?" I snicker. "I like that. Better than a good

girl, isn't it?" I start pulling my towel, as he tucks his tongue into his cheek, his knee bounces a little harder. I step back inside, holding up a finger. "Wait a minute."

His eyebrows raise. "What'd you forget?"

I pause, watching his gaze, remembering the first time I saw him, the way he caught me, made me feel confused and excited at the same time, the way he always knew just what to say. Then I remember the way he touched Susy at the gym, like there was already something going on between them, the way he kissed her in the shadows of the club, tasting her lips and running his hands all down her body.

I tuck the towel back in. "I didn't forget anything. Except that you're a dickhead." I reach for the doors and slam them shut.

Click.

On the other side, he shoots out of the chair. "Hey! What the hell are you doing?"

"What the hell am *I* doing? What the hell did you think *you* were doing last night? At the Library?" I shout through the door. "Did you really think you could get away with this?"

I reach for his cell phone and balance it gingerly on the door handle. "Why don't you call *Susy* to get you out of there, asshole? Oh, I forgot, your phone's in here, isn't it? Bummer!"

"Isa! Stop it. Open the door—we'll talk about it."

I pick my dress up from the bathroom floor and begin putting it on in the dark. "There's nothing to talk about. I was stupid, that's all. I fell for your stupid tricks."

He pounds on the glass, and the phone falls. "Isa! Open the freakin' door, come on! Don't do this!"

I straighten my dress and reach for the balcony light switch. I flick it on and off quickly to attract plenty of attention, leaving the lights on at the end of the show. "Tell your audience I say hi. Gotta go."

I slip on my sandals and pull Andrew's watch close to my face. 9:05. Perfect. He's probably waiting already. Mmm, these strawberries are good.

"You're a fucking bitch, you know that?" Andrew shouts into cupped hands at the glass.

At the door I pause and look around the room. I could take that painting. Nah. I've done enough damage. He's not worth it. I see Andrew pace the balcony, hands at his hips, then he hurls his shoulder at the door and glares at me. I turn up the one finger that best expresses how much I give a shit and close the door.

Head up, eyes focused on the end of the hallway, I strut out of there. The elevator opens, and I breeze past an elegant old couple getting out. Eleven stories down, the doors again slide open, and I head straight through the lobby.

I take a deep breath. "There's a naked guy out on a balcony!"

For a moment a multitude of eyes falls on me. A few scoffs, a few laughs. Then dozens of people rush past me to the hotel courtyard.

Exiting the revolving front doors, I drop my head and

laugh. At the bottom of the driveway I see a car waiting with hazards on. I speed up and pull open the passenger door.

"¿Y?" Stefan asks, throwing the car into first.

Getting in, I lean my head against the headrest and let out a deep breath. "Done."

Twenty-two

I called Jonathan this morning to let him know I won't be working the last week of camp. When he asked why, I came close to telling him about Andrew and Susy, just to expose them and make them look like weasels. But I decided against it, giving my mother's illness as an excuse instead. Jonathan wished us both well. Now I have nothing to do all day but watch TV and ponder my unexciting future. Hey, at least I'm with my mom.

"Isabelita, telephone." Mami pokes her head into my room.

I put the TV on mute and pick up the phone. "Hello?"

"Isabel, hi."

Great, it's Susy. "What do you want?"

"Can I talk to you a minute?"

"You're talking, aren't you?"

She sighs. "Look, I know you're pissed, but there're things you don't understand." She pauses for a response. Why, I don't know, because I won't encourage her by actually speaking back.

She goes on. "I know this sounds crazy, but it was just . . . it was just sex, that's all. He really likes you. All he does is talk about you. He's in love with you."

"In love with me?" I laugh a crazy laugh. "Do you realize what you're saying makes no sense? If he loved me or even liked me at the very least, he wouldn't have done what he did."

He wouldn't have called me a fucking bitch, either.

"How long have you been seeing him, anyway?" Before she can answer, I add, "No, you know what? I don't want to know. I don't care about the details. I'm over him. You can have him."

"About a month."

Figures. A month is the longest she lasted with Iggy, too.

"Look," she goes on. "I don't want him. I just called to see if you could give him another chance. Please. He really *is* a nice guy—he just knew you wanted to wait a while before going all the way with him, so I guess he looked somewhere else in the meantime."

"What?! That's the biggest bullshit I've ever heard, Susana. What, is he going to explode if he doesn't wait a few weeks? Whatever happened to porn sites and baby oil? Look, do me a favor, don't talk to me ever again and tell Andrew I say the same."

"I told you his agenda was different. I tried telling you, but you didn't want to listen."

"No, if you had something to tell me, you should've said you were screwing him, and I would've dropped him right there, but you kept that from me too. I'm hanging up now. The two of you deserve each other. Bye."

I would've been more of a bitch, but my brain just won't allow it. She's not worth the trouble. As for Andrew . . . *He looked somewhere else in the meantime.* Ha. Did I really love him? Or did I just love the idea that a guy like him was so into me? Whatever. Hey, I'm fine, I survived, I'll be smarter next time.

Sighhh. Fresh air, please!

I leave my room to look for Mami, eyeing the storm-girl painting in the living room with a smile. She's in the kitchen, chopping onions for the *sofrito*. As long as I live, I will never make dinner preparation seem as effortless as my mom does. It's an art form in its own right.

"*¿Cómo te sientes?*" I ask.

She lifts the cutting board and slides the onions into the saucepan with the knife. Ah, the lovely sound of sizzling. "I feel better. *Mush* better."

I laugh and squeeze her shoulders. "*Qué bueno.* You look it."

"Well, the therapy is going well. My body is accepting it."

What's different about her? There's something . . .

"Isa, I wanted to speak to you, *mi vida.*" She hands me the green pepper and a knife.

189

English. She's been speaking in English a lot more lately. "Okay." I carve out the stem and slice the pepper in half.

"When does orientation start?"

"At Michigan?"

"Yes." In goes the tomato paste.

"*El treinta y uno de agosto*. In two weeks." Man, I'd love to be at orientation, but hey, first things first. I keep chopping.

"*Bueno*. Have you bought any sweaters yet?"

What is she getting at? "Sweaters for what? What are you saying? That I should go? I already said I'm not leaving you."

She stops chopping and looks at me, a bittersweet smile at her lips. "You're leaving."

"What?"

"*Isa, mi amor querido*, I'm going to be fine. The sessions have been going very well. I have Papi *y* Stefan, and you have a life you need to start living."

"But what if there aren't any dorms left?"

"We'll find you an apartment, *no te preocupes por eso*."

"But I—"

"*¡Ya!* There's nothing to discuss. It's what you want, it's what your father and I want, and it's what Stefan wants too. *El quiere tu cuarto*."

"Stefan wants my room?"

"Tomorrow morning, we will look for coats. You're going to need a good one *en el frío de madre ese! Coño, la verdad que* you had to pick a school in the coldest place you could find. *La verdad que hay veces que creo que lo estás haciendo a propósito . . .*"

She's complaining again. Back to normal. I guess I really can leave now. Holy . . . I'm going to Michigan? "But Mami—"

"No 'but Mami,' *nada*. You always have to go against everything I say, don't you?" She smiles.

"I can't believe this. I'm leaving in two weeks?"

"Isa, if it will get that boy out of your head. *¿Pero sabes qué?*"

"*¿Qué?*"

She stirs in the ground meat for the *picadillo* and sighs. "My mother died because she wanted a decent life for me, and that's all I want for you, too." She doesn't look at me but out at the patio. Or maybe not even that. Who knows where she really is. "Just don't forget who you are . . . where you came from. Okay, *hija?*"

As if I could forget! "Of course, Mami."

Is this for real? If so, there's so much to do. I have to start packing, go clothes shopping. I'm leaving! It *is* for real! If Mami's fine with it, then so am I. It'll help close the book on Andrew, too.

"*Gracias*, Mami. I love you so much." I scoop the little pile of chopped pepper into the pot and kiss her cheek. She touches the spot with a satisfied smile. "I gotta tell Carmen!"

I rush into my room, click open Outlook, and create a new message:

From: Isabel E. Díaz
To: C. Díaz-Sanders
Subject: AAHHHHH!!!!!!!!

Carmen, guess what? I'm leaving!!!!!!!!!!!!!!!!!!!!!!!!!

That should be enough exclamation marks.

Twenty-three

Should I, or shouldn't I? Oh, what the heck.

From: Isabel E. Díaz
To: Roberto Puertas
Subject: All moved in

Hey Robi, how are you? It's beautiful up here. My apartment isn't too far from campus, so the walk won't be too long. E-mail or call me anytime you want. I hope we're still friends. Sorry about the whole Andrew thing. You were right, he was a jerk. I guess I had to see it for myself. Take care.

Love, Isa

There. I left the door open for him. If he wants, he'll get back to me. In fact I know he will. We've been friends for way too long for him not to. I click "send" and watch my message sail off into cyberspace.

It's only been three days since Papi went back to Miami, but already I have a care package from my mom. I haven't even started classes yet. As if she didn't leave me enough rice and frozen *platanitos*. I sign for the box, then hurl it onto my cheapie sofa . . . *my* sofa, in *my* living room, in *my* own apartment.

I look around for my keys (to my own apartment) and find I'm sitting on them (on my own sofa). I puncture the packing tape and slide the key between the box's flaps. There's packing peanuts, newspaper, and an assortment of things every good little *cubanita* will need while living in the harsh, Sedano-less environment of an American college town.

Packages of little *merengues*. I love these things. *Dulce de guayaba*, Cuban crackers, lots of black beans. Vicks VapoRub? Napkins? I absolutely can't live without a stack of thirty Wendy's napkins, now can I? A jar of roasted red peppers and some *azafrán* seasoning for all that *arroz con pollo* I'll be making. The little doll from the Cuba Expo. Ah, here's the stuff—a Cuban coffeemaker and vacuum-packed brick of Café Pilón.

What's this? Could she have wrapped it in any more paper? I unfold the flat, rectangular item. And there, in a nest of tissue, sits my old painting of the egret, along with a mini American flag from Sedano's. There's a note attached:

194

I'm sending you this little bird to keep you company.
Besitos,
Mami
P.S. Llama a Robi, por favor.

Jeez, a woman with a mission! She doesn't know that I already beat her to it.

Behind the painting I find something else—a large manila envelope with something hard and flat. I unclasp the flap and pull out a mini Cuban flag with a framed photo. Not just any photo. She sent me *the* photo. The one of my grandparents holding each other, squinting under the Caribbean sun. Their house, clothes, and smiles gleam from an era washed away into the sea, a Cuba of Varadero days and Tropicana nights.

"It's okay, *abuelos*," I tell them. "Your deaths weren't in vain. We're happy, we're safe."

I take the stuff to my bedroom. The photo goes on my night table, the flags here in my pencil cup, and the egret painting, I hang above my bed. I lie there for a while looking at it. It seems so out of place here in the land of pine trees and snowy winters. But after staring at it for a while, I close my eyes and float into a peaceful sleep.

I dream of swamps and saw grass, anhingas and herons, humidity and storm clouds . . . and the sweet scent of the approaching rain.

Gracias a las siguientes personas who helped make this book happen:

My editor, Leann Heywood, and my agent, Steve Chudney, for believing in me and for your expertise. People will read my stories because of you. I'll always be grateful.

Yolanda Triana, for being the greatest mom and making me fill out college applications so I'm not still a cashier somewhere . . . oh, yeah, and for spell-checking my Cuban Spanish; Oscar S. Triana, for knowing when to be *un payaso* and when to be a dad; Chris Núñez and the Wednesday night group for your awesome (and applied) contributions; Oliver González, for reading every chapter and telling me it was good; Michael González, for taking long naps; and my entire family, for being patient and supportive.

And to Nana and Dadi (Matilde Andreu and Orestes Figueredo), wherever you are. I bet you never thought everyone would have a copy of that snapshot hanging on their walls seventy years later, now did you? Thanks for making me a Cuban Being.